FORGED

STAR BREED: BOOK TEN

ELIN WYN

HAKON

"I cannot imagine what the Emperor was thinking, sending someone like you on such a delicate mission."

Ambassador Thalcorr sniffed and took a small, disapproving sip of his tea.

Everything he did was disapproving, so I didn't take it personally.

"It may not be our place to understand," I answered mildly. "All you have to know is that we've both been assigned to go to this Station 112 and make contact. You'll talk to the corporate envoy, and I'll follow-up on the manufacturing order." I grinned, happy to know the sight of my teeth made him nervous. "Speculating on more than that doesn't do either of us any good."

ELIN WYN

Of course, I'd done plenty of speculating on my own.

Quinn and Torik's foray into the Areitis Sector hadn't gone unnoticed by Vandalar.

As Emperor, he had other Imperial fish to fry, but I was certain that as soon as he had the time, he'd be redirecting his attention, and troops, towards reestablishing control in the sector.

"Why do we even need to make an order from a second-rate corporate manufacturing facility?" Thalcorr demanded.

Again.

I fought back a sigh, instead taking a sip of my own drink.

It definitely wasn't tea.

"It's not so much that we need it," I explained. Again. "Any of the Imperial manufacturing facilities could provide the same part. Think of it as a good-faith order. A test."

And it worried me more than a bit that the ambassador couldn't understand such a basic opening gambit.

I'd asked Quinn to do a little poking around. It didn't look like Thalcorr had done much more than attend parties for the last few decades.

Maybe Vandalar was trying to reward him with an actual assignment.

Or, more likely, punish him for some political infraction I didn't want to know about.

"I'm not here to get in your way. I'm just along to make sure everything is built to spec."

And to ensure that Desyk Consolidated Systems was at least slightly legitimate.

Lorcan and Cintha's little adventure into the world of coerced and kidnapped workers had us all on alert.

So when our friends from Heladae had sent out a message on the dark boards of Areitis, just to see who might be willing to open talks with the Empire, it was just our luck that the one nibble we had so far was from a corp that didn't have the cleanest reputation.

Vandalar had limits.

Nice change from the usual political nonsense.

"I have served the Empire for my entire career," Thalcorr started up again.

I didn't doubt it. Every inch of Ambassador Rix Thalcorr looked like a patrician, Hub-born fop.

Silvered hair carefully swept back at the temples, smooth, perfectly regular features, tall but not too tall, thin but not scrawny.

I'd lay good credits the man had never missed a meal in his life, or used his muscles in anything other than a sculpting pod.

I pushed away from the table and got to my feet,

anxious to interrupt him before the spiel picked up speed.

"Look, we don't have to like each other. To be honest, I doubt if we ever will." A raised eyebrow confirmed his agreement on that point, at least. "But you need to trust that Van knew what he was doing when he sent me on this mission."

"That's a level of faith that I'm struggling with," Thalcorr muttered under his breath.

"And, whether I like it or not, I have to trust that he has some belief that you're minimally competent. At least, I'm crossing my fingers."

And with that, I took my beverage and headed back to my cabin.

It actually had been a pleasant hour in the lounge before ambassador stick-up-his-ass had found me and begun complaining, for the sixth time in six days, about the mission.

I swiped my hand over the palm-lock of the door and went into my cabin, twirled the chair around and plopped down, pulling up our progress on my own tablet.

Two hours left until I could actually get off the ship and do my job.

I made another tally mark on a private document.

One more time I'd managed not to throw the arrogant prick out an airlock.

It was the little victories that counted, right?

———

We are approaching Station 112. Please prepare for docking.

Finally. No one who'd ever traveled on the *Queen* could say the Imperial ship *Kodo Ragir* was cramped. But any more time cooped up with Thalcorr, even on something the size of a dozen residential hives, was going to end up with Vandalar short one ambassador.

I pulled up the exterior cameras on my tablet, threw the visuals to the wall screen, and winced.

Station 112 had seen better days.

A long, bulbous spindle held most of the vital machinery, and a hub wheel extended from the most central bulge.

The 'foot' of the spindle flared into another disk, with radiating ports for docking. Below the docks, the station continued for another several yards of deck, which finally curved into a dome.

Zooming in, the metal looked scarred and pitted, and far too many lights blinked erratically.

"What the hell have you gotten us into, your Imperial Majesty?" I grumbled.

But I shouldn't complain. I'd volunteered to head out on this sideways scouting mission.

Getting Orem Station back into shape after Granny Z had taken it back had been a long, slow job.

Sure, securing our home base was important, especially after what had happened to the *Daedalus*...but it'd been too long since I'd been in the field.

And it had to be said — the company might suck, but the food on an Imperial ship couldn't be beat.

A gentle shudder through the hull told me we'd docked. Time to see if this little gamble was worth the roll.

At the airlock, Thalcorr preened, chin raised, foot tapping impatiently, waiting for the atmosphere to cycle.

I stayed back, just in case any last-minute urges came over me.

Finally, the door unsealed and irised open to reveal the short, shielded walkway leading into the station before us.

"After you," I waved. If there was paperwork, he was welcome to it.

And there was always paperwork. At least, if you came in through the front door.

This time, Void help us, there was an actual welcoming committee.

"Ambassador Thalcorr! Mr. Hakon!" The portly young man actually bowed, still bouncing on his toes in excitement. "I can't tell you how much your visit means to me, and to Desyk Consolidated Systems!"

Thalcorr shot me a smug smile before returning his attention to the official. "On behalf of his Imperial Majesty, let me say how pleased I am to make your acquaintance, Mr…"

The official kept grinning, curly brown hair in disarray around his round face. The older man behind him rolled his eyes, but stayed quiet.

Thalcorr coughed gently. "My tablet must have had an error. I don't have your name, Mr…"

"Oh!" the poor man flushed but recovered quickly. "Commander Serrup, leader of Station 112, at your service." He fumbled in his pocket, then handed each of us a plastic card. "You'll need these."

"How very nice, Commander Serrup," Thalcorr oozed without bothering to ask what he'd just taken. "I'm so anxious to see your facility. Perhaps you could take me on a tour?"

"Of course, of course!" Serrup burbled. He glanced at me. "Aren't you coming?"

"Actually, I'd like to see where our parts are being manufactured."

His eyes widened. "But the order is almost completed." He looked at the man behind him, and got a quick nod of confirmation. "There's not much to see."

"Still. That's where I'll start. I can find my own way."

"I suppose," he said doubtfully, but before long, he and Thalcorr headed towards the main axis of the station, ready to see whatever sights there were.

The second man stayed behind, watching me with cautious eyes, his expression carefully blank.

"Please tell me you're actually in charge here, and not that idiot," I said.

His lips twitched. "It could be worse. Shan Alcyon, station operations." He held out a hand. "Commander Serrup is one of the cousins of Desyk Consolidated Systems' CEO."

"I see."

YASMIN

"**K**illing yourself over that schematic isn't going to get you out of here any sooner, kiddo," Tinon said, stretching at his barely touched workstation.

Theoretically my supervisor, it seemed like most of his time was spent telling me how *not* to do things.

Specifically, not to work so hard.

Probably because it made him look bad.

I glanced at my station timer.

It read 5018 hours left.

"It might. If I can adjust this part of the mold just a bit, it'll save me on the material fee." I pulled up the diagram on the tablet, rotated it, tweaked it again. "See?"

He rolled his stool over, his bleary eyes almost clear

enough to feign interest. "That's clever," he admitted. "But you know…"

I chimed in with him. "The company always gets you in the end." Crossing my fingers, I sent the part to print.

He leaned back, pulled up the next job on his tablet and started poking at it halfheartedly. "Running late with a project will wipe out any bonus you get for using fewer materials."

"I know," I muttered, pulling on the microgoggles as the printer beeped. "That's why I'm trying to focus on it." Zooming all the way in, I checked the thickness of each section of the finished sample.

The part wasn't anything special as far as I could tell, just a redesigned particle flow distributor for long haul engines.

I'd done a dozen projects like it in the months since I'd accepted a contract on Station 112.

But none of them had landed on my tablet with an 'urgent' tag before.

"You hear more gossip than I do," I said, still examining the part. "Any noise on the wheel as to why Serrup is all hot and bothered about this gig?"

Tinon snorted. "Potential new client, maybe a big one." He spun out the program to replicate his parts, sent it to the fabricator without checking anything, and shut down his bench again. "Though I can't imagine where in the sector they found a poor slob desperate enough to do business with Desyk."

With a loud whoosh, the door to the lab slid open.

Startled, I fumbled the sample, then stared up at the mountain of a man standing before me, who had caught it before it hit the hard floor.

"That's likely to be me," the man said mildly, looking around.

He couldn't have been answering Tinon.

For one thing, the labs were soundproofed.

For another, I couldn't imagine anyone further from my mental picture of a 'desperate slob' than the man who now stood in the middle of the room, filling it with his presence.

It almost looked like he was wearing an exoskeleton, except that obviously he wasn't. He just was naturally taller and broader at the shoulder than anyone I'd ever seen. He had black, raggedly cut hair and dark eyes that I'd bet didn't miss much.

And right now, those eyes were fixed on my sample as he rotated it slowly in his massive hands.

"Can I have that back?"

He turned it over again. "You modified the spec," he rumbled. "Why?"

Alcyon stepped beside him, scowling. "We'll have her compensation docked, and another tech assigned to the project."

The giant held up his hand. "Nope. Not until I have an answer."

I shoved the goggles back, snarling a little as they caught in my hair. "Because the original design was flawed, that's why." I pulled up the specs, then my modifications. "Look at this. Your output valve was far too large to have any sort of control. You would have flooded the fuel chamber in minutes if you'd installed these as is."

When he smiled, his entire face changed. Scary became stunning. "Good catch."

I rocked back, studying him. His charcoal gray pants tucked into boots and khaki shirt under a black jacket, didn't look like an engineer, but there was something about his tone of voice.

"You did that on purpose, didn't you?" I spun back to my work bench and flipped through his specs again. "What sort of maniac sends deliberately flawed specs?"

"Apparently, this kind of maniac," he grinned, and tossed the sample back to me.

And at that moment, I saw something interesting enough to forget my annoyance.

In the breast pocket of his jacket was a thick plastic card, with just enough showing for me to see the red stripe running down the side.

"Insulting important clients is a fast way to get your

hours docked, Miss Joi," Alcyon stated. "You may want to proceed carefully."

Gripping the edge of the bench, I forced myself not to snap back. There were more important things to think about now.

The giant raised his eyebrows, watching me, but I stayed silent.

"If we're done here, Mr. Hakon," Alcyon said, "let's continue on our way. We'll start with the hub, the center of the workers' social life around here."

"I'd be happy to give you a tour, if you'd like," I offered in my best perky voice. "Give you an actual worker's point of view of things."

Tinon looked shocked but didn't say anything.

Smart man.

"That will be quite enough, Miss Joi," Alcyon barked.

The two turned and walked out the door.

I braided and re-braided the end of my hair, thinking, finally throwing it back over my shoulder as I got back to work.

Fingers flying, I punched in the commands to start mass fabrication of the flow distributor.

I hadn't found a flaw, the client hadn't found a flaw, good enough.

I stood up and tossed the microgoggles on the bench.

"I think I'm calling it a day," I announced.

"You never leave early," Tinon said, eyes wide with confusion. "You're always telling me the only way to get out of here is to take as many gigs as possible, get as many hours stacked up as you can."

"Maybe I'm listening to your advice for a change," I said, shrugging. "You're always telling me the company wins anyway, so why work so hard?"

He didn't look convinced, but I didn't really care.

Halfway to the hub, I stopped the turbo lift and glanced down at my coarse gray coveralls.

Standard wear for the station, all from the fab labs.

I hadn't thought about bothering with anything nicer since getting here.

But maybe it was time to be a little more strategic.

"Capsule level D4," I commanded the lift, bracing for the tiny lurches as it shifted direction, away from the hub and towards the personnel levels, such as they were.

After the door slid open on my level, I went to the communal replicator, then stopped cold, lost in the options.

I'd been away from high society for far too long, and had barely been interested even before everything in my life turned upside down.

But I still would bet from the way Alcyon was happy to take time out of his schedule to escort the newcomer around the station, he was someone important.

And 'important' meant money. Always did.

I flipped through the clothing options, wincing at the prices.

Like everything else here, I'd pay for it in hours deducted from my total.

But it couldn't be helped.

I flipped past screen after screen of short, shimmery dresses.

Not my thing. Besides, the giant, Mr. Hakon some-one-or-other, would have seen plenty of skin before.

And to be honest, mine wasn't anything special.

The next set of screens showed more dresses, but this time with bows and ribbons and poofs.

If that was his style, I was out of luck.

'Cause I sure wasn't wearing any of it.

Not even for a handsome man like that.

Ooh.

That would do.

I pressed my thumb to the pad to finalize the transaction and in minutes, I gathered my new outfit to my chest, climbed the short ladder to my capsule one-handed, and crawled in.

A yard and half square and two yards deep, the shelf bed ran down the length of the wall, with storage beneath.

Not exactly the most comfortable of homes, but it was expected you pretty much would be working or in the hub. The capsules were just for sleeping, or maybe watching a vid. Nothing else.

Quickly, I unbraided my hair, smoothing it back and banding it, then wiggled into the long black pants. The silky, flowing fabric was strangely soft against my legs after months of the rough, coarse coveralls.

The sapphire blue top wrapped in the front, making a v-neck, not too low, just enough to be suggestive, and belted with a wide black sash. Best of all, the draping sleeves had just enough of a fold to make a perfect tiny pocket.

Once upon a time, I might have outlined my eyes in gold shimmer, put more gold on my lips.

But there were only so many hours I was willing to burn on this little project.

Grabbing the last item from my nearly empty storage bin, I hurried back down the ladder.

Back in the turbo lift, I braced myself.

The noise and clutter of the hub grated on both my ears and my nerves.

Always had.

But if that's where Alcyon had taken the stranger, that's where I needed to go.

Stepping out of the lift, I surveyed the crowded space. Even in the dim light, surely the giant would be easy to find. He'd stand head and shoulders over everyone here.

But I didn't see him. Not by the tables clustered around the arches of greenery, not by the units dispensing whatever kind of relaxer you had a taste for.

Maybe they'd moved on to the games.

It seemed unlikely Hakon would want a tour of the private booths... and if so, I was out of luck.

Heading deeper into the swarm of people, my stomach growled at the enticing smells.

I didn't spend much time here. The replicator on the capsule floor was programmed for basic dishes. They were cheaper, and nobody expected you to be social.

But they certainly weren't good, by any definition.

Suddenly, a meaty hand grabbed my left upper arm. I spun, pulling away from the balding, beady-eyed man blocking my way.

"Hey, pretty lady, haven't seen you here before," he said, leering at my cleavage. "New to the station? I'd be happy to give you a personal tour."

The gods of irony were apparently making an appearance tonight.

"She's not new, Urtu," a woman's nasal laugh cut through the air.

Maybe irony wasn't the right word. Petty annoyance?

Irritation?

Could I make a sacrifice of someone to them?

"Hello, Grilla," I smiled, making an effort for it not

to be a mere baring of the teeth. "How are you doing tonight?"

The blonde rolled her eyes. "You'd know if you ever hung out with anyone. But no, you're too good for the rest of us drones." She leaned back against the chest of the man she was obviously with. He didn't seem to be following the conversation, too focused on what her hands were doing in his lap.

"I have never said that," I countered.

Sure, I'd thought it plenty of times, but never said it.

At least, I didn't think so.

"I'm just trying to get my hours in, same as everyone else. Hours in, contract worked off, back home. That's the deal, right?"

Urtu's hand tightened on my arm, tugging me towards the table. "Looks like you're taking the night off. Why don't you spend some time with us?"

Right hand fisted in the folds of my pants, I braced, ready to strike.

Then a shadow loomed over the table.

"I don't think she wants to join you," my missing giant said mildly. "And I really think you should let go of her arm."

He paused, and even Grilla's hands stopped moving.

"Now."

HAKON

The little man jerked his hand back as if Ms. Joi had caught fire.

Good.

I held my hand out to her and waited.

"Shall we?"

"I thought you'd never ask," she said, instantly ignoring the trio seething at the table behind her.

We passed through the crowd in silence, moving with the ebb and flow of people.

Some were dressed in the gray coveralls that seemed to be the station uniform, but more people had changed into casual clothes, or seemed dressed for a party, silk and sequins flashing everywhere.

I glanced down at Ms. Joi. Her breathing was even,

only the slight flare of her nostrils a clue as to her emotions within.

"Thank you," she said softly. "I don't often come out this way. And since you rescued me, please call me Yasmin."

There was a story there, but I could let it wait until later.

"You can pay me back by being my guide. Alcyon got a ping to go help Commander Serrup with some crisis and had to abandon me."

She bit her lip but said nothing.

"I had the feeling it wasn't an uncommon occurrence," I continued, waiting for a response. From the moment I'd seen her, I knew this woman had secrets.

And secrets were what I was searching for here.

"I'm sure I wouldn't know," she glanced up at me, deliberately fluttering her long dark lashes. "I'm only a lowly fabrication technician. It would be impossible for me to hear the gossip about how incompetent our station commander is." Another flutter of lashes. "Completely, absolutely impossible."

"That's what I thought," I said. "But it seems like a lot of people for someone with, shall we say leadership challenges, to be in charge of."

We had reached the far side of the open space, another cluster of replicators and beverage dispensers surrounded by high tables filled with laughing, drinking, workers.

"It helps that expectations are low," she said, a wry smile lifting the corners of her mouth. "Besides, we're all pretty motivated to get our hours in. Or at least, those of us that want to get off this place."

I watched the groups at the tables around us. Behind the laughter, more than a few had a hollow, desperate look about the eyes.

"Why would that be difficult?" I asked.

But before she could respond, her stomach growled, and her cheeks burned crimson.

"Let's get some dinner and you can tell me all about it."

She shook her head quickly. "I'm fine, really." She waved at the replicators. "I can pick up something later, closer to my quarters."

"Well, I'm hungry," I said, walking over to see what was on offer. It wouldn't be the same as what was offered on the *Kodo Ragir*, but honestly, I wasn't used to such rich food anyway. "I can't imagine you'd make me eat alone, would you?" I teased.

She sighed, and showed me how the replicators were set up. Fairly close to Imperial standard, slight differences in the options.

Not surprisingly, there were a number of dishes that I didn't recognize. I started to click one of each.

At the end, Yasmin moved her thumb to the small block square, and I caught her hand. "I'm hungry, I'm paying."

"I doubt if you're set up in the system," she argued. "Did they take your print?"

I fought back a grimace and started deleting food from the order. There was no reason for her to pay for my curiosity or my appetite.

"But," she continued, tilting her head to the side, "they may have set up credits on your card. Can I see it?"

After a moment, I realized what she meant, and pulled out the access card Serrup had handed me. She waved it above the screen and the total zeroed out, blinking green.

"Perfect," she breathed. For a moment, the intensity in her eyes took me aback, but then she blinked, and the strange look was gone. "Here, let me show you what's good. If you're still hungry, you can try the rest of it." She shook her head. "If you really want to."

"I should probably take that back," I said, and slipped the card back in my pocket.

In the end, I ordered anything that made her eyes light up. Not exactly as much as the previous order had been, but maybe I didn't really want a double order of *perrs rado*, given the way Yasmin's nose wrinkled at the thought.

The replicator dinged and slid open to reveal a tray filled with bowls of steaming… something.

"I'll get this," I grabbed it. "You lead on, find a table in this mess."

All we could find was an unoccupied booth in the corner under one of the arches.

"Thank you for the meal. Will your legs fit under the table?" she asked, running her eyes up and down my frame.

"Probably," I grumbled, wedging myself in. "If not, I'll find someone to volunteer theirs."

I took a bite of everything, but made sure to push the small bowls back closer to her side of the table. If my food was free, I'd bet hers wasn't.

"So how come so many people are here? Shouldn't they be working or something?"

Yasmin shrugged, swallowed another bite of the spicy vegetables. "Shifts run around the clock," she answered. "A lot of people do their minimum hours, then don't worry about it. Not my style, but I don't have to worry about anyone but me. I want to get my hours in, take on as few debits against them as possible, and get out of here."

Interesting. I thought about it. Not exactly slaves, more like indentured contracts, with the odds stacked high against ever completing them.

That was more than Alcyon would have told me.

"There's got to be more to the station than fabrication labs and this."

She leaned back, hands over her stomach. "For that meal, I'll even show you my favorite place on the station." She gathered the empty bowls onto the tray and waited for me. "Come on, I think you'll like it."

In the turbo lift, I took a moment to study her. She was interesting. Obviously smart or she wouldn't have caught the design defect I'd deliberately introduced into the file.

But there was something hidden behind that careful smile.

The lift paused in its glide, changing directions from horizontal to vertical as it carried us through the station.

I shifted my weight as the faint scent of pholla trees tickled my nose.

"Anything wrong?" she asked, a slight crease between her dark brows.

"Nothing at all." Must have been something else. I'd only seen pholla trees on one mission, about as far from the Areitis Sector as I could imagine.

It'd been years ago, but the sweet, clean scent was unmistakable.

And impossible.

The minutes ticked by in the lift. "Where are we

going?" I asked. "Seems like there shouldn't be much this far from the central hub."

"All the way to the bottom," she said. "Are you afraid of heights?"

Definitely interesting.

The door slid open and we approached a heavily secured hatch. "Through there?"

"Not a chance," she answered. "Secondary control room. I'm not certain even your card would get you inside." Her eyes flicked to the card reader, considering. "No, the observation dome is just this way."

As we walked, I could feel the slightest pressure in my inner ear as the deck's artificial gravity adjusted to keep us upright, even though from my memory of what the hub had looked like, we were pointed down.

Relatively.

"Here we are," she said and swiped open a door with her own card.

The dome before us was clear plexi, filled with the swirling, muted pastels of the gas giant below.

Chairs were scattered through the room, all turned to face the breathtaking spectacle.

But no one was there but us.

Yasmin stood still, transfixed by the sight. "That's Tocarth 5. No matter how many times I've come down here and watched it, I've never understood why they put this here," she finally said, voice soft and wondering. "It doesn't do anyone any good, doesn't make a profit." She shrugged, rubbing her upper arm. "Maybe the station architect decided there should be one thing of beauty in this place."

She stepped closer to the plexi, and I watched her, as curious about her as I was about the station I'd been sent to investigate, then she wrapped her arms around her torso and shivered.

"Are you cold?" I asked.

She glanced over her shoulder at me. "I know it's silly, station temperature is constant no matter where you are. But there's something about looking into the Void that always chills me just a bit."

"Here." I shrugged out of my jacket and wrapped it around her shoulders. It swallowed her, hanging almost to her knees.

"Thanks." She walked up to the edge of the plexi and pointed. "Do you see here? That swirl of purple and red?"

I stepped closer, watching the planet below, wondering what I was looking at.

"It's a storm that's raged for thousands of years, with no signs of slowing down. Everything we do, everything the corps have ever done, is a flicker of time as far as that storm is concerned." She laughed quietly. "Well, if the storm was aware of anything."

I watched it for a moment, streaks of what looked

like white clouds swirling and crashing with the violence of an alien ocean.

The silence grew between us and I glanced down to find her stifling a yawn.

"You said everybody worked around the clock here?" I carefully placed one hand on her shoulder. "When did your shift start?"

"More hours ago than I'd like to think," she admitted. "But there are more places I could show you."

"No, I'll have my official guide do that." If he's ever off babysitting duty, I thought. "If you don't mind, I'd like to see the workers' quarters, then we'll call it a night."

She tilted her head, eyes narrowed. "I'll show you the outside of my quarters," she said dryly. "But that's it."

My face burned as I realized how she must've interpreted my words. "No!" I blurted. "I mean yes. The outside! That's all I meant."

She laughed, handing me my jacket as we left the observation dome and reentered the lift.

Moments later, the door slid open and she bowed forward, arm waving in front of her in a grand gesture. "Our final stop of the tour will be the capsule level D4."

Both walls of the hallway were divided into a grid, each square a little over a yard on a side, stretching on until the corridor curved out of sight.

A few steps from the lift, Yasmin rested her hand on the wall, and I realized the slight indentations in the surface that ran vertically between each column were a series of ladders.

I glanced down the hall again, calculating.

"These are all micro capsules? How many workers does the station hold?"

"Only a few thousand," she said, shrugging "It's not that there's so many on the station, they just don't have much space to allocate for workers' quarters."

That was interesting.

On a station this size?

They could have raw materials and fabricators stacked in a dozen cargo bays and still have plenty of room left over.

What did they need the extra space for?

YASMIN

"Work, dammit," I whispered as I pressed against the side of the corridor.

Usually, no one came down to the observation dome.

But with my luck, tonight would be the night someone decided to move the party out of the hub.

For the fourth time, I swiped the hastily cloned access card across the reader. I'd never tried to use the cloner without watching my hands before, but Hakon had been only mildly interested in the gas planet below.

A twinge of guilt and regret ran through me. He'd seemed like a nice man.

No. That wasn't exactly right.

He seemed like a dangerous man, but with a sense of honor.

Someone I might have liked getting to know, once upon a time.

But time wasn't something I had a lot of anymore.

And certainly not right now.

PING!

"Dammit," I whispered.

But no one seemed to notice the happy chime of the secondary control room as it slid open for my illicit explorations.

I hurried inside, sliding the door closed behind me and studying the control panel.

Not one I was used to, but I'd be able to figure it out easily enough.

First step, block any notification that the access point was in operation. Commander Serrup ran a sloppy station, but Alcyon was no slouch.

If it hadn't been for his over-the-top security protocols, I would've been finished with this mission months ago instead of trapped here, making endless widgets while I looked for a way into the company's records.

Task completed, I started carefully working through the files, learning their structure.

Orders for parts and fabrications, internal comms about delays in supplies.

Quotas and complaining.

Reprimands and excuses.

Billing, shipping, threats from other divisions of Desyk Consolidated.

But nothing that I needed.

I didn't feel an iota of guilt ransacking their system, looking for their secrets. If I was successful, Serrup would be recalled. Alcyon might lose his job, might be reassigned.

Either way, it was nothing compared to what Desyk had done to us.

Somewhere, buried deep within the system would be the secret of Station 112.

What I'd come here to find, what I'd sold myself into a contract for. And when I found it, I could finally go home.

Home.

My chest tightened, thinking of it. Thinking of what it used to be.

But I shoved the unproductive, traitorous thoughts to the back of my mind, locked them away, and focused on my task.

PING!

I whirled around, but my explanations and denials faded away at the sight of Hakon, leaning against the wall.

Yup. There it was. The flash of danger behind those dark eyes.

"Apparently you don't need too much sleep to get

rested up, ready for a round of late-night espionage," he said mildly, his quick glance taking in the room, the activated consoles and screens displaying row after row of filenames.

"What are you doing here?" I asked, chin high. "This doesn't seem like the sort of place a guest would be interested in."

He stepped further into the room, as the door slid shut behind him. "But I'm the one with the access card." Hakon held it up. "At least, the original one." His lips twisted into something almost like a smile as he slid it back into his pocket. "I was wondering why you were so eager to show me around. Now I know, don't I?"

My cheeks burned a little.

It hadn't just been that.

For the first time I could remember, I'd enjoyed an evening. Eating together, talking about nothing much.

Just his company.

But the mission came first.

"You had something I needed. I don't know whose side you're on. What other choices did I have?"

"You could've asked for help," he offered. "That might have been a better option."

A bitter half-laugh burst from my lips and I turned back to the console.

"Either stop me or let me work," I said. "That's all the help I need."

"Give me one good reason I shouldn't send a message to Alcyon," he said. "Void, even half of a good reason. Try!"

My back stiffened and I turned slowly. "What do you think I have been doing ever since I got here?" I spat the words out, heedless of the fact that they would mean nothing to him. "I am trying. I am trying to do what I need to do, regardless of the consequences."

He stepped toward me, his hand outstretched. "Tell me what's so important," he argued. "If you —"

With a crash, the control room shook, knocking me to the deck.

Or would've if Hakon hadn't dived forward to catch me, holding me so tightly I couldn't help but notice his strange, spicy scent.

A second later, the room rocked again, and the screens flashed red as alerts spread throughout the station.

"If I didn't know better, I'd say the station was under attack," Hakon said. He frowned at me. "Or is it?"

I wriggled, squirming to get out of his grip. "Let me see!" I insisted.

He released me and I rushed to the console, slapping at the keys until it brought up outward-facing cams.

On another screen, I spliced into the communications network.

Against the dark outside, a sleekly curved ship hung in space, smaller craft ranged to each side.

"Why are they here?" I breathed, my mind reeling at the sight.

The *Foil* and her full escort. They should have been anywhere else but here.

Hakon came to my side, studying the screens. "You didn't call them?"

"Of course not," I snapped.

Then another shot rocked the station, not a direct hit, just enough to throw all the systems into a tizzy.

The communications channel sprung to life.

"As you have undoubtedly noticed, we have only fired warning shots so far." The stern, lined face of a tall dark-haired man filled the screen, then the camera panned out to show a younger man standing a bit behind him.

Arrayed behind the pair were three more men.

Corporate negotiation specialists, Uncle Ran had always called them, laughing.

Soldiers, specializing in particularly violent negotiations.

And he should know. He was standing on that deck, issuing commands for the surrender of Station 112.

And my brother, my trusted friend and confidant, stood at his side.

I shook my head, focusing on what they were saying.

"Consider this a hostile takeover," Ran continued. "You have 15 minutes to surrender the access codes and sign over all rights to the station and its processes. Otherwise, we will be forced to start taking out targets in earnest."

"I don't understand," I said, hands shaking just a bit. "What's going on?"

"We've got to go. Now," Hakon said, eyes fixed on the screen.

He turned away from the console and grabbed my shoulders. "Whatever your mission is, it's clear this wasn't part of your parameters. You're not going to do anyone any good if you stay here and get killed."

"No," I said, the steel in my voice surprising even me. "I have a job to do. This doesn't change that."

If anything, it made my timeline even shorter.

I could find that file. I could find it and deliver it to my uncle.

Same plan, just accelerated.

Fifteen minutes.

No one would be watching internal security with the ExaTek flagship right outside.

I wouldn't have to try to be sneaky about it.

"Is it worth—"

With a beep, the communications screen reactivated

and split to show the both the bridge of *Foil* and the Command Center of the station, as Serrup started rambling on about his rights, about corporate sovereignty, about how important he was.

It would have been funny, if he wasn't actually in charge.

Uncle Ran liked word games. In another mood, he would have cheerfully ran verbal rings around Serrup until the poor fool ended up swearing allegiance to ExaTek while still believing he was faithful to Desyk.

But from Uncle Ran's tone, this wasn't one of those times.

Alcyon stood beside Serrup, no doubt whispering lines that Serrup refused to parrot.

A third man stood to the side, tall with silver hair brushed back at the temples.

"Dammit," Hakon growled. "What is Thalcorr doing there? Why isn't he back on the *Kodo Ragir*?"

I glanced over at him. "Who is he?"

"Even more of a pain in my ass than you are," he snapped. "And unfortunately, my responsibility." He studied the screen. "I haven't been there. What's the fastest way?"

"Use your access card, tell the lift 'priority override', Command Central." I turned back to my own work and shut off the comm channel.

I couldn't afford the distraction.

Somewhere, no matter how well hidden, were the files I needed.

And despite Hakon's arguments about wanting to help, I was clearly on my own.

As usual.

HAKON

I should have thrown her over my shoulder and carried her out of there.

Instead, I went tearing up to Command Central, waiting for the blasted lift to make the ascent.

Void, I could have climbed through the decking faster than their 'priority override' speed.

But all the while, I kept seeing that face.

Not the old man with his threats.

Or the young man standing beside him who bore a disturbing similarity to Yasmin.

But the merc standing in the back to the left.

Jenke.

Not the best angle, but surely, that was Jenke.

Somehow, I needed to get over to that ship. Ideally, without being fired on.

But by the time I reached Command Central, it seemed more likely that Jenke would be heading our way as part of a boarding party.

Serrup's eyes nearly popped as he ran from one console to the next. "Why don't we have weapons?" he shrieked. "Are you saying we can't defend ourselves at all?"

"We're a small manufacturing station." Alcyon stood still in the middle of the room, watching his nominal supervisor with narrowed eyes, not even bothering to hide his disdain. "Having weapons would have made us a target earlier. The risk wasn't worth it."

"But *I'm* worth it!" Serrup yelled, pushing an operator out of the way, desperately looking for something, *any*thing that would save him.

"You!" He whirled on Ambassador Thalcorr. "Doesn't your ship have weapons? Why aren't you doing something to save us?"

I stepped between the idiot and the ambassador.

It might have been tempting to let them hash it out, but then I'd have to explain it to Vandalar.

Or worse, Ronan.

"The *Kodo Ragir* is lightly armed, nothing near what would be needed to take on the flotilla you've got outside."

Ambassador Thalcorr stepped to my side, nose in the air. "Additionally, we are here on a diplomatic trade

ELIN WYN

mission only. This appears to be an internal sector affair between two legitimately recognized entities. We have no cause to be involved."

Huh.

Maybe the old man had more spine to him than I'd thought.

Serrup lunged towards Thalcorr, but backed away at my growl, deciding instead to run in circles around Alcyon again.

"Internal affair or not, maybe you should get back on board the *Kodo*," I suggested quietly.

Thalcorr sniffed. "Apparently the docking mechanism was the target of the first attack. Our ship won't be able to tether safely for some time." He nodded his head gracefully. "Our captain is working on other plans. And I am certain that a peaceful solution to this situation can still be achieved."

I scoffed. "How certain?"

He watched the circus of Serrup and Alcyon playing out in front of us. "Moderately. If necessary, I can assist Mr. Alcyon in sedating Commander Serrup."

The screens flashed on again.

Same view.

Old man, young man. Mercs in the back.

And Jenke.

No doubt about it.

"Is this room set up for a two-way holo-broadcast?" I whispered to Thalcorr.

"Yes," he said dryly. "I'm certain you're about to see our host's negotiation skills shortly."

"The clock is ticking, gentlemen," the old man said. "Have you come to a decision?"

Serrup moved closer to the screen, hands waving wildly. "I don't understand why you're doing this," he whined. "I know ExaTek already has manufacturing centers that can do everything we can here."

Alcyon moved next to the babbling Serrup, edged slightly in front of him.

"Greetings, Chancellor Denau." He bowed slightly.

Quietly, I moved behind the pair, far enough back to be unnoticed, but close enough that the cams would catch me.

"I am afraid that we are unable to comply with your request on such short notice," Alcyon continued blandly.

I knew the moment Jenke saw me.

His eyes met mine, widened slightly.

But as I was about to try to signal him, his lips pressed tightly together and he looked away.

Alcyon was still droning on. "With more time, I'm sure that we can come to an arrangement that would be to the mutual benefit of both of our corporations. Perhaps we could — "

The old man, Denau, cut in. "The arrangement will be exactly as I stated. As you are obviously unsure of my seriousness in this matter, I'll have to give you a token of my good faith." A flicker of a smile. "I'll start with the bottom of your station. From the specs I've seen, directly above that are your worker capsules. Unless they're willing to reassign their contracts to my corporation, they're no good to me anyway. If I keep working my way up the spindle of your station, how far do you think I can get before you have a critical failure?"

He gestured to someone off screen. "The clock is now accelerated. Five minutes until you start losing parts of your facility."

The screen cut off.

I fell back, mind whirling.

The bottom of the station.

Where I'd left Yasmin.

Who'd turned the comm screens off.

Jenke would have to wait.

I fell back, next to Thalcorr.

"You certain you've got this handled?" I asked.

"I believe so," he said as we watched Alcyon's security team filling the bridge, slowly circling Serrup, who was too hysterical to notice them.

"I am confident that Mr. Alcyon will see reason."

"That's good. I need to get back down to that dome."

One elegant eyebrow rose. "I had understood that your team had a tendency to rush into danger, but that seems extreme."

"There's someone down there," I grunted.

Thalcorr's face changed, for once a deep line wrinkling his forehead. "Then what are you waiting for, young man? Go!"

Tearing back to the lift, I waved the access card. "Observation Dome, Priority!" I snapped.

If anything, the car moved even slower this trip, as if willfully distracting me.

Maybe it was just in my head, knowing the countdown until the dome was shattered, until Yasmin was cast into the Void.

But it didn't really matter.

"Void take it!" I snarled, and ripped open the control panel. "Stupid safety overrides…"

That was more like it. I held tightly to the wall as the lift screamed through the track, coming to a jarring stop at the lowest level.

And the clock in my head kept ticking.

"Yasmin!" I roared as I dashed through the short corridor. "You better be done with whatever you're doing!"

The crash of the ceiling panels falling to the floor with the next impact drowned out my shouts, sparks flying as the volley began.

Throwing panels out of the way, I ducked under a tangle of loose wires blocking the entrance to the control room.

"Yasmin!"

She stood over the console, back hunched, legs braced against the buckling of the deck. "I've almost got it!" she yelled over her shoulder. "I just need a minute more."

"We don't *have* a minute!" I dodged forward, grabbing her by the waist.

"Wait!" she yelled, bashing at the panel until a datachip popped out. She grabbed it, sealing it in the side pocket of her coverall pants.

"We're going now!" I growled, pulling her with me as we headed back to the lift. Explosions popped and crackled behind us.

"Run!"

YASMIN

Diving through the data, all of my focus had been on the mission.

Finding that file.

But with a snap, reality shifted, and I realized we were in real danger.

Sheets of metal had fallen, littering the deck of the secondary control room. Twisted wall panels exposed sparking wires, and imminent disaster was everywhere.

I looked around frantically. "What's happening?" I blurted out.

Hakon shook his head. "I'll tell you about it on the way out," he said. "Move!" He shoved metal out of the way to clear a path back to the corridor, and I hurried to follow in his steps.

"That ship is firing on us, that's what's happening."

He wrenched the door open, and we slid through. "So far, they're either still getting the range or playing with Serrup."

"Oh, he'd have the range already figured out the instant they arrived," I answered absently as I hunched and twisted to avoid another hanging bunch of cables. "They're playing with us, no question."

"Huh," was Hakon's only reply.

I grabbed at his shoulder for balance, then froze. "If I can get to the Command Center, I can stop this!" I cried, swallowing.

Probably.

Except, I didn't know why Uncle Ran and Luca were here, so far ahead of schedule.

But surely they'd stop when they knew I had the data.

"Alright then, I'm not exactly enjoying being stuck in a shooting gallery," Hakon said.

He pulled the door of the turbo lift open and we dashed inside, shouting orders.

I eyed the mangled metal on the side of the car.

If I didn't know better, the lift's control panel had been clawed open.

"Don't ask," he growled as, with a groan, the lift headed up again.

"Wasn't planning on it," I answered.

He'd been remarkably good about not asking me too

many details. Surely, I could extend him the same courtesy.

"But whatever you did, we need to get back up the spindle, fast."

Except, despite the priority override code, despite whatever modifications he'd made, the lift only rose a fraction, then shuddered, starting and stopping in a jolting cycle.

"Give me a minute," Hakon said, then reached into the wires, splicing and twisting them into patterns that I was fairly certain had not been authorized.

Then with the screech, the car surged upward.

I crouched down, holding onto the wall for balance.

"Told you it'd be—"

With a thud and a clatter, something hit the roof of the car.

And then we fell.

"Hold on!" Hakon shouted.

"To what?" I hollered back, but he was busy ripping back the access panel in the ceiling of the car.

The opening was covered with a pile of debris and bent permasteel. Clinging to the edge, he shoved it to the side to clear the way.

He hoisted himself out, then lay on his belly on top of the still-falling lift car, arm outstretched for me.

"Take my hand!" he shouted.

"Are you crazy?" I yelled. "Where can we go from there?"

"Don't know yet, but it's gotta be better than stuck inside a little box waiting to hit the bottom!"

That was a point in his favor.

Shakily, I pushed myself up and reached for him.

In an instant, he'd swung me out of the car, holding me tightly to his chest with one strong arm.

The sides of the lift shaft flew past us as we descended, almost too quickly to focus on.

"It won't be long before this thing hits the bottom," Hakon said. "Keep holding on, okay?"

"Wait, what?"

Instead of answering, he jumped.

I didn't have time to do more than squeak before his free hand had wrapped around the guide rails I'd barely been able to see.

I risked a glance below. The lift car was still plummeting away, no more than a speck now. "What do we do now?" I whispered, already feeling exhausted.

"We climb," he said grimly. "You go first; I'll be right behind you."

"You just want me to be the first to get hit with whatever falls down," I teased.

"Be a hell of a lot harder for me to catch you if you fall, if you're already lower than I am," he shot back.

Second point to him.

And somehow, all of his points involved me falling to a grisly death.

"I don't think I like this game," I muttered.

"Why not?" he said from below. "Think of it as giving me a behind the scenes tour of seldom seen parts of the station."

I snickered, and hoisted myself up one more time. The rails were studded at regular intervals with small openings, just big enough for me to squeeze my foot in.

Sort of like the world's worst designed ladder.

I couldn't imagine how Haakon was managing.

Maybe, if he was lucky, he'd be able to get a toe into those little openings.

I couldn't see what he was doing, but however he was managing, he didn't seem to be having any troubles staying right behind me.

It didn't take long to realize that what had knocked the lift car down also had completely blocked the shaft, just a few decks above us.

"I think whoever is on that ship is doing a bit more than just taking out the observation dome," Hakon said. "How are you doing?"

I leaned against the rail, giving my aching arms a moment's rest. "I don't think we're going to make it to the Command Center," I said. "Even if I could climb that far, I don't think we can get through all of that."

"Alright," he said. "Time for a new plan."

I chewed my lip. "I've got a ship," I admitted reluctantly. "But I'm not sure how we can get to it. If we can, I can hail the—" I caught myself just in time before I named my uncle's ship. "The attackers, see if we can do a better job of negotiating than Serrup."

"Last I heard," Hakon said, "the docking mechanism isn't working."

I tapped my fingers against the rail, thinking fast, not liking any of the answers. "My ship isn't exactly in the docks, or anywhere station security knows about. But if I can get to my quarters, I should be able to maneuver it to the docks remotely. Probably even without the assist from the station."

"Really," he commented blandly. "And what makes you sure about that?"

I stared at the blocked lift shaft again. Maybe I could twist through it, not have to do this.

But it didn't really seem likely.

"Because that's how I got it here," I ground out. "I came in on the recruiter's shuttle, brought my own ship in behind me. It's been cloaked against the station's side for months."

Hakon's laugh boomed through the shaft. "I can't wait to tell Alcyon how crappy his security is," he finally managed. "What other little holes have you found?"

"Not enough," I confessed, still irritated by my failure. "But for now, can we focus on getting to my quarters?"

"First, we'll need to see where we are," he decided. "Let's keep heading up until we see the next pair of lift doors."

Thankfully, it wasn't far. My arms had gone from aching to screaming, and my efforts not to look down had made the muscles in my neck stiff.

But I wasn't done yet. I had to climb past the doors in order to give Hakon space to work. Leaning precariously away from the rail, legs wrapped tightly around it, he easily wrenched them open.

"Any luck?" I called down. "Can you see where we are?"

"Not where we wanted to be," he grunted, then leaped through the open doors. "Don't recognize it at all. You'd better come on down and take a look."

Wearily I climbed back down, but at the sight of the deck beyond the lift doors, a new wave of energy ran through me.

"Not my quarters, but workable, completely workable." Then my excitement faded. The lift rails were set back far enough in the shaft that I couldn't see how he possibly could have made the jump. And as for me... "But how do I get out there?"

Hakon wrapped one hand around the edge of the

door and leaned forward as far as he could, with the other hand outstretched.

It didn't reach me.

Not even close.

"Jump. I'll catch you."

My brain couldn't even process the words.

"I promise, I'm not gonna let you fall. Trust me."

My throat closed up.

I didn't trust. That was a rule.

But he'd kept me alive so far.

And as far as he knew, I was the only way we had out of this situation.

I might not be able to trust, but I'd always been able to count on enlightened self-interest.

"Alright," I said. "One, two, three!" Flexing my legs, I sprang as far as I could towards his hand.

It wasn't far enough. I wasn't going to make it!

My scream barely had time to echo before he snagged me out of the shaft, pulling me close to his chest.

"Alright there?" he rumbled, one massive hand carefully smoothing down my hair. I stayed buried against his chest for a moment, willing my heartbeat to get back in line.

"Yes, I'm fine." I pushed away and looked up at him, but his face seemed carefully blank.

Right, then. Just in my head.

"Where are we?" he asked.

"The maintenance deck." I nearly danced down the corridor in excitement, skipping around fallen panels. "And do you know what's fantastic about being on the maintenance deck?"

I hadn't been assigned a shift on this deck, maintenance wasn't what my contract specified.

But I'd checked it out a few times, just to be sure. You never knew what might be useful.

Hakon grinned. "Nope, but I'm pretty sure you're about to tell me."

"They've got a secondary airlock to get out to the station's hull for repairs."

"And that helps us how?"

"Because with an airlock, they have to have suits," I explained as I worked my way down the corridor, hoping the built-in lockers wouldn't be blocked. "And with suits, we can just jet to the ship, easy as it can be."

"Easy?" he echoed doubtfully. "That'd be a nice change."

"Here they are," I said, pulling open the locker door to expose a rack of environmental suits. "Hurry up and get dressed," I said, unlacing my boots and tugging the pants leg over my coveralls, wriggling a bit as I pulled the suit over my hips.

"Not gonna do me any good, Yasmin," Hakon said. "There's not a suit in there that's gonna fit me."

My hands froze midway through sealing up the chest plate.

"Alright," I said, thinking frantically. "Time for a new, new plan. We're not that far from my quarters from here. There are maintenance shafts, with proper ladders, that we can use to get there."

Hakon gently sealed my wrist cuffs around the gloves and checked the power pack and the jets. Then he triple-checked the oxygen levels.

"You go out, get to your ship. I'll be fine," he said.

"That's a terrible plan," I snapped. "What do you mean, you'll be fine? You won't be fine without a suit!"

A grin curved the corners of his mouth. "That almost sounded like you care," he said. "And I don't even have something you need."

I turned my back, ignoring him so I could think of a new, new, new plan.

Maddening, impossible man.

"I mean, I'll be fine modifying one of these suits to fit me."

I spun back to him, eyes narrowed. "How the hell do you think you're going to manage that?"

"I'm pretty clever at these little projects," he shrugged. "But I'll need a few minutes. By the time you get to your ship and bring it back here, I'll be ready."

Oh.

That made sense.

Sort of.

"I'll be back as soon as I can."

I swallowed hard, then deployed my helmet.

The clacking of the material as it unfolded and stiffened into place around my head, visor shimmering to transparent, muffled anything he said in response.

But he stood by the first airlock door with one hand on my shoulder, and even through the thickness of the suit, I could feel the warmth of him.

Probably I just imagined it.

He nodded sharply and pressed the button to open the inner door.

As it sealed behind me, I waited, counting, staring out through the porthole into the sliver of black.

By the time I hit twenty-five, the outer door slid open, exposing me to the vastness of space, and the swirling colors of the planet below.

For a moment I stared, mesmerized.

Then I shook myself, clicked off the magnetic field in my boots, and launched myself into the Void.

It was amazing. Like flying, free from anyone's eyes or restraints. Until a flicker of light out of the corner of my eye caught my attention and brought me back to reality.

Uncle Ran was still taking potshots at the station.

If I was lucky, I'd have time to play later.

Right now, I'd better focus on getting the job done.

Carefully controlling the jets, I skimmed the surface of the station, riding up the metal skin until it flared out in the middle, beginning the bubble that housed the Command Center.

It was there that I'd decided was the best place to hide my little runner, when I started this mission so many months ago.

Only the faintest shimmer gave it away, pressed into the curve of metal, almost completely out of range of the cams that surveilled the station's exterior.

If anyone had been paying attention, they'd have caught me swooping in.

But at the moment, they had more important things to worry about.

At least, more potentially lethal things.

Reversing the jets, I braked just in time to drift within hand's reach of my ship.

There.

Although, if you trusted your eyes alone, my hand would seem to have caught in midair, hanging on nothing, I knew what I touched was real, despite the interference from the cloak generator.

Hand over hand, I worked my way to the hatch and punched in the code, and like the revelation of a magician, my ship appeared.

"Finally, we're getting out of here," I muttered as I opened the canopy and slid into the pilot's seat.

Technically, there was a single back seat. It was small, and I wasn't entirely certain how comfortable Hakon would be when I picked him up.

If I went back to pick him up…

A niggling thought crossed my mind.

The mission was the most important thing, right?

I was here, I had the ship, I had the data.

The smart thing to do would be to go straight to the *Foil*, report to my uncle that the mission was a success, and get out of this damn system.

Try to forget I'd ever heard about Desyk Consolidated and Station 112.

Except…

Hakon had saved me.

More than once.

He didn't even need to come back and find me when the attack started.

My hand paused over the ignition sequence.

Why had he?

Because he was a decent guy, I answered myself. Which is why I was going to go and get him.

Enough of my honor had been stolen. I refused to sacrifice any more.

Slowly bringing the systems back online, I released the magnetic locks that had kept my ship so securely nestled against the station's hull and, with the gentlest puffs from the thrusters I could manage, pushed away.

Then another problem struck me.

I had no way to communicate with Hakon.

Surely, he'd be able to see my ship from inside the airlock, right?

He seemed confident about rigging up a suit that could fit him. I shook my head. I didn't see how, but he was just arrogant enough that I half believed he could do it.

And if he couldn't, well, I'd wait as long as I could for him.

But when I reached the airlock, I realized there was no need to wait.

Through the small viewscreen, I could see the outline of his dark form next to the outer door, already waiting for me.

Almost worse than his arrogance, seemed to be the fact that it was justified.

Carefully maneuvering my ship, I got as close to the outer door of the airlock as I could.

We'd time it carefully, so it'd be like a dance.

Then the airlock opened, and I gasped.

Frantically, I slapped at the controls to open the canopy, any thought of grace long gone.

Because Hakon hadn't exactly done as he'd promised.

Instead of modifying a suit so that it would fit him,

he'd ripped the back and helmet modules off one of them, but ignored everything else.

As he launched himself towards me, I tried not to remember anything I might know about how long skin could survive in the freezing Void without permanent damage.

One one-thousand. Two one-thousand.

Three—

Then he was in, and I lowered the canopy behind him so fast that it nearly pushed him down into his seat.

When the canopy was sealed and the cabin filled with oxygen, I punched the control to unfold my helmet and took a deep breath.

And let him have it.

"What the hell did you think you were doing?" I snapped as I turned to stare at him.

He hunched over in his seat, helmet already back, power pack, jets, and oxygen slung over his shoulder, not looking a bit worse for wear.

If anything, that arrogant grin was broader than ever before.

"I told you I'd be fine."

I turned back to my controls.

There was no reasoning with him.

"Whatever. Let's get out of range from those shots, and see if we can get anybody to listen to us."

Carefully, I eased us away from the hull, flicking on my communication panel.

"*Denau's Runner* to *Foil*. *Denau's Runner* to *Foil*. This is Yasmin, requesting a clear channel to the bridge."

But we got nothing but static back.

"Maybe we're getting interference from Station 112," I muttered and started moving us further away.

Far enough to see the blast from the *Foil* take out the observation dome entirely.

But not far enough that we could avoid the shattered wreckage that filled the space around us.

As I whipped my little ship back-and-forth between the wreckage, Hakon stayed silent behind me, letting me focus on trying to keep us alive.

Until "Watch out!" he shouted.

But it was too late.

HAKON

"Yasmin!"

"I'm on it!" she snapped back, voice echoing in the tiny craft, working the controls desperately, fighting against the uncontrolled spin.

That last jagged piece of the dome's wreckage had done a number on us.

Long and curved, it had sent a spider web of cracks across the ship's canopy and knocked the thrusters out of alignment.

We spun wildly, flickering glimpses of Station 112 and the gas giant Tocarth 5 passing in and out of view, over and over until they almost blurred together.

"Get your helmet back on and reverse thrusters," I shouted. "Do it now!"

But she didn't answer.

Dammit.

Yasmin's head lolled to the side.

I reached over the back of her seat, triggered her helmet back on, and checked her oxygen.

She was breathing, both tanks in the green.

But until I stopped our mad spin, the G forces would keep her unconscious.

And there was only so much pressure the human body could take before irreversible damage would start.

"I know it's your ship, baby, but I think you better let me drive," I apologized as I gently pulled her out of the front seat, pressing uncomfortably close to her in order to change positions.

She was so small, so determined to be tough. And so fragile underneath the bravado.

Reluctantly, I pulled my hand away from her shoulder and settled myself uncomfortably in the pilot's chair.

"Ship, report status," I barked, hands too full with the controls to pull anything up manually.

All systems appear to be compromised, a bland voice replied.

Void.

I never thought I'd miss Nixie.

"Cut starboard rear thruster fifty percent, adjust the rest to compensate."

As the thrusters slowly decreased the speed of our

stomach-churning barrel roll, I pulled us around to the other side, gritting my teeth against the Gs.

It was starting to be unpleasant, even for me.

I had to get Yasmin out of this.

Navigation systems are eighty percent restored, the ship reported.

"That's fantastic, what about communications?" I forced out from between gritted teeth.

Communication systems are still off-line at this time. Have a nice day.

Well, we wouldn't be calling for help, not from Station 112 or the *Kodo* or from that attacking flotilla that Yasmin seemed to know a little too much about.

After we got out of this, she had some serious explaining to do.

But first, I had to make sure we got out of this.

Finally, I could see straight, could guide the craft in a limping, jolting way.

"We can do this," I called over my shoulder to the unconscious Yasmin. "It'll take us a while, but we can get back to the station. We've got enough air that my ship can pick us up from there."

Even without comms, the *Kodo Ragir* would feel obliged to rescue a ship in distress.

Useful thing about working with the Imperials under Vandalar's new moral code.

Then the crack across the canopy spread a little further.

"New plan," I muttered. "What does that make, Yas, four new plans now? Or are we on five? You can tell me when you wake up."

I pulled up the navigation system, scanning quickly for options.

We weren't going to make it back to the station.

I glanced down at the gas giant as it rapidly filled more and more of my vision.

Also not a good idea.

There, just past the horizon... What was that?

"Computer, does the planet below us have any moons?"

There are thirteen objects designated as moons of Tocarth 5.

"Which one of them is the closest, and does it have an atmosphere we can breathe?"

For optimal results, please ask your questions one at a time.
Alright.

We were getting out of this, Yasmin was going to tell me what was going on, and then I was gonna get her a ship with a decent AI.

And seats with better legroom.

I took a deep breath.

"What is the name of the closest moon?"

The navigation system highlighted the moon that was just coming into range.

That moon is designated Sat 9.

"Show me all known information about Sat 9."

The screen filled with data and I flipped through it as quickly as possible.

A little low on oxygen, but survivable. Not a lot of information in the file, but at least it didn't seem to have walking trees or carnivorous vines or anything crazy.

At least, nothing reported.

"Alright, Yas, let's see if we can make it."

Slowly, painfully, I goosed us towards the moon.

"Looks like a thin upper atmosphere," I told Yasmin. "Probably cold at night, but with luck, it will make it a little less rocky getting down there."

"What?" she asked blearily.

"Great, you're awake for the terrible part."

"What?!"

She was definitely awake now.

We burned through the thin atmosphere, and I fought to keep our nose up.

"This ship isn't rated for landfall!" Yasmin shouted over the screams of tortured metal.

"We're not rated to survive in the Void without a ship," I answered. "It had to go one way or the other."

A golden red expanse filled the canopy, and the spider web of cracks spread even more.

We shuddered and rocked in the seats, rocketed back-and-forth by the turbulence.

"We're still coming in too steep! Reverse thrusters, now!" I commanded, and smashed the buttons.

With a jolt, we were both slammed back into our seats.

But with the ship's systems so crippled, I couldn't tell if it would be enough.

"Impact coming in, three, two..."

And we hit.

Yasmin's yells melded with the screech of metal as the ship slid on its belly across the desert floor.

"Why aren't we stopping?" she shouted.

"Physics!" I answered back

I couldn't think of a better answer. There was one, I was certain of that, but at the moment, I was far too worried about the cliffside we were racing towards.

"I don't think we're going to stop in time," Yasmine cried.

She was right.

"Keep your helmet on," I yelled, triggering my own, then I hit the button to eject the canopy.

It ripped away from the body of the ship with a tremendous whoosh.

We were slowing, but still not enough.

And the cliff wall was growing bigger every second.

"Stand up, babe," I said, and pulled her tight to my chest, pressing my helmet to hers to make sure she could hear me. "Just hang on, and it will be over in a minute."

"That sounds disturbingly final."

If I didn't do this right, it could be.

I waited, watching as we slid closer and closer to the cliff.

Still faster than I would've preferred. I'd be able to take the brunt of the fall, but she'd still be jolted.

But there wasn't any choice anymore.

"Time to go!"

Wrapping her tightly in my arms, I sprang from the edge of the cabin, at a sharp angle from the careening ship.

With a thud, my shoulder hit the hard packed desert floor and we rolled over and over, until we were well clear of the ship's path.

As soon as we stopped rolling, I propped up on one elbow, triggering her helmet release and catching at mine.

Her eyes were wide.

"Let's not do that again."

"If you insist," I shrugged. "Not really on my list of top ten experiences to revisit."

She rolled over and we both stared at her ship.

The nose had crumpled into the cliffside almost all the way back to the cabin.

"We might've survived," she said slowly. "Maybe."

"Pretty sure my legs would be broken by now," I said, heaving myself up from the desert floor and reaching down to help her up.

"That would be hard to deal with, I suppose," she said. "I'm a terrible doctor."

"That's alright. I'm a terrible patient."

Slowly we walked, or rather limped a bit, to better examine the damage to the ship.

My jacket was shredded, and my pants weren't in much better shape, but the environmental suit had done a better job keeping Yasmin safe.

"Where are we, anyway?" she asked.

"You're not-very-helpful ship's AI identified this as Sat 9."

She looked at me blankly.

"It's one of the moons of the gas giant," I added.

She stopped cold. "That's a completely uninhabited moon. I wasn't even sure there was an atmosphere there. Here. Whatever. Who's going to be able to find us?"

"Well, most important question first," I said, continuing my slow, sore way towards the wreckage. "Obviously, there's atmosphere. It's a little thin on oxygen, but not dangerously so."

She hurried to catch up. "Alright, we can work with that. There's got to be enough left of the ship that we can get a message off to," she glanced at me, looked guilty. "To someone."

More secrets.

"That seems likely, especially considering how thin the atmosphere is. We shouldn't get much interference."

I placed a casual hand on her arm, turning her slightly towards me. "But it might be helpful if I knew who exactly we were signaling."

I tried to keep my voice level, even. But obviously I'd stumbled into some sort of complicated game. And not only did I not know the rules, I didn't even know the players.

She bit her lower lip, large worried eyes searching my face

"Could we start with you telling me more about where you're from?" she finally said. "Maybe while we're checking my poor ship for anything that survived you ramming it into a cliff?"

Not exactly what I'd hoped for. But maybe trust had to go both ways.

I continued walking. "An information trade, that seems reasonable enough. For now, let's see what we've got to work with."

When we reached the ship, I realized it wasn't quite as bad as it looked.

It was still pretty bad, though.

"This is never going to fly again," she said mournfully.

"Seems unlikely," I said. "Tell me there are emergency supplies, a replicator hidden somewhere, anything useful?"

"It's a stealth ship," she snapped. "Not a luxury cruiser."

She hoisted herself up into the cabin and started digging around what was left of the footwell in the front.

"Here, let me get that for you." I just pulled the entire seat out. It was easier, and gave her more room to work. And we weren't going to be flying away anytime soon. Not in that ship.

It was the logical thing to do, but still, probably a mistake.

She stared at me. I shrugged.

"It started rocking pretty hard when we descended," I explained. "It seemed an easy bet it wasn't that firmly attached anymore. And right now, everything is pretty much scrap."

"Sure," she replied, voice doubtful.

I carried the seat into the shade of the cliffside and leaned it against the rock.

By the time I came back, she'd opened a small hatch in the ship's deck. "Some emergency rations,"

She offered up a box. "I didn't really expect I'd need them, but enough to get us through a few days."

"Anything's better than nothing," I said. "I'll have one later. What else can we use from here?"

In the end, I moved both seats, most of the communications equipment, and a pile of miscellaneous components into the quickly lengthening shade of the cliff.

"Night's coming soon," I commented. "We should think about shelter."

Yasmin looked around. "I'm not seeing a lot of possibilities."

There really wasn't much to see. The desert stretched out endlessly, dotted with low, silvery green brush.

No rocks big enough to shelter under, except for the cliff that ran off in both directions. I'd be able to scale it to the top, not a problem.

Yasmin wouldn't. We'd either need to make our way out across the desert, or pick a direction to explore and keep walking along the cliff.

Both options would have to wait until tomorrow.

And they didn't help at all with the problem of freezing temperatures tonight.

"I wonder..." I muttered, studying the sad, stripped down craft.

It wouldn't be comfortable, I finally decided. But it might work.

"You're not emotionally attached to what's left of that ship, are you?" I asked Yasmin.

She snorted. "I'm emotionally attached to surviving. Tell me what you're thinking."

YASMIN

It was obvious we both had our secrets, I thought as I cut the fabric and upholstery off the pilot and passenger seats with a sharp piece of permasteel.

The evening was hot enough, I'd pulled off the top of my coveralls, wrapping the sleeves around my waist. No pretense of high fashion, not anymore.

Hakon had ripped the seats from the mangled body of the ship without even trying hard.

He'd torn off another, larger piece of permasteel, and was now using it to hack through the desert floor at the side of the wreck.

The destroyed jacket and slightly better-off shirt had been tossed to the side, and the interplay of muscles across his broad back kept catching my eye.

I shifted, turning away so I wouldn't keep being so distracted.

This wasn't the time or place.

But he was very, very distracting. My thoughts kept returning to how it had felt to be wrapped in his arms.

Safe, secure, even though every time seemed to be right before we were about to do something terribly dangerous.

"Ouch!"

I stared at the blood welling from my finger, and instinctively put it in my mouth.

Or tried to. Hakon had materialized by my side, his massive hand wrapped around my wrist. "Let me see that. We don't know if there's anything in the dirt here that might infect it."

"And how are you going to tell?" I shook my head.

"I'm not, but that goes on tomorrow's list of projects," he answered. "For now, let's just rinse it and wrap it."

My coveralls had survived more or less intact underneath the environmental suit. Hakon took the makeshift knife from me, and with surprising gentleness, cut away a small piece from one of the loose arms tied at my waist.

"I'm almost done with the trench," he said.

I shook my head, confused at his speed, then realized how much longer the shadows had crept from the cliff into the desert. "I must have zoned out for a bit, sorry." Blushing, I crossed my fingers, hoping he wouldn't ask exactly what I'd been thinking about.

"Lucky for us both, it's almost time for dinner, then bed," he announced. "We'll both be in better shape to deal with things in the morning."

While he finished ripping apart the seats, I pulled the tabs on the rations, waited for them to heat, and poured out a bit more of our small reserve of water.

"I really hadn't planned on an extended stay anywhere." I arranged our dinner on a flat rock. Then rearranged it. Then moved it all around again.

Nope. No matter what I did, it didn't look like enough.

Glancing up, I watched Hakon take the upholstery and the fabric to his trench.

He'd explained his plan to me, but it seemed too far out to be possible.

Except, apparently, he was doing it anyway.

"Dinner's ready!" I called out. Maybe there was a way to give him more of my packet. I'd seen how much he ate… when was that?

Just hours ago, it seemed, back in the hub. While back on Station 112, artificial lights gave us the luxury of determining whatever schedule we wanted. On an actual orbiting body, we were tied to the real cycles of day and night.

It was like when I was a kid, the times we'd been able to get planet-side and go camping as a family.

Staring up into the darkening sky, Tocarth 5 looked bigger than ever, the swirling pastels filling my vision.

Dad would have loved it here.

"Hey," Hakon said quietly. "What's wrong?"

Sitting back up quickly, I dashed the tears from my eyes. "I must be more tired than I realized," I said brightly.

He frowned, but didn't press.

Another point to him, and we weren't even in a life-threatening situation.

At the moment.

The rations almost counted, though. "They really want to make sure you only eat these in a true emergency, I guess."

"I don't think anyone is going to opt for this over a replicator," he agreed. We quickly finished and washed the terrible taste with sips of the water.

"Tomorrow, we'll have to look for water, too," he said.

"Actually, I have an idea of where to start." I pointed to the desert. "Too dark now, but some of those little shrubby things were taller than others. And the bigger ones looked almost like they were growing in lines."

He frowned. "As if someone had planted them there?"

"No," I shook my head. It seemed so clear, but somehow, I was having trouble getting the words out. "They're spaced too irregularly for a farm, I'd think. But it might be that the bigger ones are getting water from an underground source."

Hakon nodded, thinking. "Worth investigating, for certain. The list for tomorrow keeps getting longer."

I stood up, stretching. "Neither of us got much sleep last night. And not for anything fun, either."

My cheeks burned. How had that slipped out?

Hakon snorted. "I don't know. If I ever need to break out of a space station again, I think I've found my partner. We showed a certain elegance, I thought."

"You're crazy," I laughed, grateful that he'd let my words slide.

He carefully packed away our trash. "Never know when something might come in handy." Standing, he headed into the desert. "I'll meet you back at the ship in five minutes. Make sure you're ready to be in for the night, okay?"

Right.

In less than five minutes, I joined him at the ship, staring into the trench. "This is…what, exactly?"

The trench was maybe a little over a yard deep, three yards long, and one and a half yards wide. It would have looked pretty much like my capsule back on Station 112, except that here, perched precariously on the far side, was the wreckage of the stripped-down ship, but turned onto its side for some reason.

"Our burrow." He pointed to one end. "All of our supplies are there. I don't know what roams around in the dark here, and we can't afford to lose anything."

He'd padded and covered the rest of it the best he could with the materials from the seats and the scraps of his jacket.

"It's still going to be a bit lumpy, I'm afraid."

I patted his arm. "It's great. Next time we crash, I'll make sure to have pillows packed." I shivered, pulling my coveralls top back over my torso. "It got cold fast," I muttered.

"And it'll get colder," he said, frowning. "Let's get in and get covered up."

He handed me in, then jumped down beside me. "You might want to go ahead and lie down." He pointed to a spot. "Over there should be safe."

"Should be?" I asked, but hurried to the place he'd indicated.

Standing in the center, he jumped up, grabbed the upper lip of the ship, and pulled it down on top of the trench.

I curled into a tight ball, arms clasped over my head, but other than a few loose pebbles clattering down, nothing fell into the trench.

Our burrow.

Now cut off from the cold night air by my upside-down ship.

"How are we going to get out in the morning?" I wondered, startled as a soft light began to glow.

Hakon finished tying the used ration package to the frame. "I'll push the ship back out of the way. Couldn't think of anything else that would keep the heat in, and honestly after the day we've had, neither of us are up for standing guard duty."

I stared at the light. "You modified the heating element. Clever."

"Won't last long, not much left after it finished its primary purpose," he shrugged. "But I thought it might help with any buried alive thoughts you might be having."

"I hadn't been having any until you mentioned it. Thanks."

He sat, resting his back against the trench wall, and patted the ground next to him. "We've been a little busy with that whole surviving thing. But maybe we should start sharing a little information. It might help."

I studied his face. The beginnings of a heavy beard shadowed his jaw, but his eyes were the same. The danger I'd imagined lurked behind them was real, no doubt about that.

But somehow, not for me.

A strange heat started in my belly. At least, not in the way I'd worried about.

I took a deep breath, tried to clear my mind as I scooted over to sit next to him. "You're on. Point for point."

"You're a little competitive, you know that?"

"My brother's brought it up more than once," I admitted.

His eyebrows raised. "Family information so soon in the game?" He nodded thoughtfully, as if just as careful with his words as I was. "Okay, I'll trade back. I have brothers, too."

"Really? Are they nearby?" I don't know why, but that little glimpse of his family intrigued me.

Unfortunately, it also reminded me of how complicated things had gotten.

Luca, standing on the bridge of the *Foil* next to Uncle Ran.

Neither of them where they were supposed to be.

I pushed the thought away. I didn't want to be upset.

Not now.

Not with Hakon so close that the trench seemed to fill with his spicy scent.

"Nope," he laughed. "Not unless someone's already sent a message back home about our hasty departure from Station 112." He chuckled, scrubbing his fingers through his hair. "Don't get me wrong, they're fantastic, but occasionally a pain in the ass."

"That sums it up," I agreed, suddenly desperate to ask more, but not wanting to answer more questions about my own family.

Hakon placed his hand over mine gently. "That wasn't so bad, was it? Two down."

"And a million to go." I swallowed hard.

The mission was all that mattered.

No one could be trusted.

But now, if I was going to get off this rock, maybe I'd have to make an exception.

"I took the contract on Station 112 to get information," I blurted.

He rubbed the back of my hand softly in small circles. "Not sure if it really counts if I'd already figured that out," he said. "Cloning my access card so you could break into their systems was kind of a giveaway."

Even in the dimming light, I could see him. Sense him.

"I guess that's true," I laughed. "ExaTek is my home corp. My family corp."

He didn't look surprised. Honestly, he didn't look like the admission meant anything at all.

Odd.

"I gotta say." Hakon turned my hand over, tracing patterns into my palm. "I'm not exactly up to speed on

81

all the corporation politics in the sector. That doesn't mean much to me, but I can tell it does to you."

An impossible thought struck me. "You're not from the Areitis Sector?"

"Nope, as strange as it is for me to say it, we're part of the Empire now."

I shifted to stare at him. "The Empire is still around?" I gasped, amazed. "From everything I'd ever read, it seemed like it would've imploded on itself, broken up into savagery by now."

His fingers found mine again in the dark, pulled me back next to him. "It almost did. A couple of times, actually. But it's pulled itself back together."

The Empire.

Still out there.

It was too much to imagine, too much to think about.

And with every burning, teasing touch of his skin upon mine, for once in my life, it was easy to put all the worries and all the plans aside.

"As fascinating as this is," I decided, "I think I'm done talking now."

The flickering light made it easy to swing myself over and kneel across his lap, until our faces were a hair's breadth apart.

"Do you feel like you have anything you need to say?" I murmured.

Hakon answered by gripping my hips, digging his fingers in and pulling me tightly against him. Groaning at the hard length of him, I brushed his lips with mine, finally flicking my tongue out, unable to resist tasting him.

"Yasmin," he whispered, then knotted his fingers around my braid as he claimed my mouth, his tongue twining around mine, the fire running through my veins building to an unbearable level.

Quickly, he flipped us, covering me with his body while running kisses and nips down my neck. The burning need consumed me, demanding more.

"Now," I gasped. "Clothes off, now."

HAKON

Yasmin was like a drug.

I'd never get enough of her.

Every moan or gasp just spurred me harder, made me crave her more.

Slowly, I unfastened the front of her coveralls, watching her delicate skin turn to gooseflesh in the cold air.

Air.

I froze, breathing deeply, her intoxicating scent enough to drive me back into her arms, to bury myself in her.

Breathing.

"Void," I cursed, and scrambled away from her. "We've got to stop, Yas."

The makeshift light had burned out, but still, I could see her glazed eyes blink, looking lost. "What? Why?"

"Because before we crashed, I was fifty percent sure you hated me."

She pushed away, refastening her coveralls, hurt and shame painted clear across her face, even in the darkness.

"Not really," she shook her head. "I just had things to do. A mission."

"And then we crashed on a planet with an atmosphere low in oxygen," I reminded her gently. "You've been taking sips from the tanks all day, but not for the last few hours. At this point, the lack of oxygen is impairing your judgment."

Stopping was almost impossible. I could still smell her, the scent of Pholla trees mixing with her arousal.

But realizing that her actions were likely due to oxygen deprivation, rather than actual attraction, set up a force field around her body that I wouldn't, couldn't cross.

"That's not right," she still sounded dazed. "That can't be right."

"Tell you what," I offered. "We get out of here, some-place where we know oxygen is not an issue, and see how you feel about things then."

"Right now, I really don't like you," she muttered. "But you're right."

"Let's get some sleep." I stayed sitting, careful not to touch her. She might have been impaired, but I knew I wasn't.

"Are you planning on sleeping upright all night?" she asked, her voice mostly back to its usual tartness. "That's ridiculous. You aren't going to be any good to either of us if you wake up tomorrow so twisted you can't walk."

"It wouldn't be the first time," I promised her. "I'll be fine."

"You keep saying that, then end up doing something crazy."

"I think I've hit my quota of crazy for the day."

With a humph, she settled down on the padded floor of the trench. It wasn't much, but it was the best we could do.

Slowly her breathing slowed and evened out, as the chaos of the day overwhelmed her.

And I was alone with my thoughts, which quickly spiraled into endless questions.

Yasmin had said ExaTek was her family's corporation. And she obviously had recognized both the older man and the younger one on the ship.

That ship was where she'd first thought to go for safety.

Did that make them her family?

If they knew she was on Station 112, her mission

incomplete, why would they open fire without demanding her return?

And speaking of family, what was Jenke doing on that ship?

More importantly, why had he refused to meet my eyes? I knew he'd seen me. We'd never been close, but it was pretty damn impossible to mistake one of us for anyone else who might be running around the sector.

Then why hadn't he responded in any way?

A soft whimper ripped my attention back to Yasmin. She'd curled up into a tight ball, arms crossed over her chest, her face scrunched up even in sleep.

"...cold..." she half-whispered.

At least that was one thing I could fix.

Carefully, I lowered myself flat, next to her.

"Here we go, babe."

If I'd thought it was impossible to pull away from her before, gently wrapping my arms around her again, easing her until she lay on my chest, knowing nothing else could happen, was worse.

After a moment, she sighed, snuggling into my chest, body relaxing into mine.

Stroking wisps of her hair back from her face, I reconsidered.

Maybe this wasn't so bad after all.

IN THE MORNING, I pushed the wrecked ship off from our burrow and breathed in the thin, cold air.

"Lots to do," I called over my shoulder to where Yasmin was still curled up, sleeping deeply.

Too deeply?

Dammit.

I grabbed one of the surviving suit tanks and released the valve just enough to start a flow of oxygen right under her nose.

Quickly she sputtered and pushed away.

"Turn it off, I'm fine!" she exclaimed.

"Take a few more breaths," I insisted.

She reached over and turned off the tank herself. "And what are we going to do when all the tanks are completely empty?" She pulled herself to her feet, a little slowly, but steadily enough. "We just need to figure a way to get a signal out. I'll be fine." She narrowed her eyes. "You say that all the time. Don't even think about fussing."

Fine.

I hauled out our salvaged parts, then reached back in to help her out.

As I brought her up, her eyes widened at something behind me.

Adrenaline rushing through me, I spun to face the attacker.

But apparently, I was a few hours too late.

"I'm glad we didn't face whatever that was," Yasmin said, leaning out from behind me.

Large oval tracks crisscrossed our camp, circling around our burrow until all the tracks blurred into a well-worn course.

Worst of all?

I hadn't heard a thing.

Obviously, Yasmin wasn't the only one affected by the lack of oxygen.

I straightened my shoulders.

Worry wasn't going to fix anything.

Action would.

"We'll have to be on the lookout for whatever that was, make sure we don't stay out too late." Scrutinizing our surroundings offered no more clues. "But for now, what do you want to tackle before it gets too hot?"

Yasmin stared out into the desert. "I think we should look for water first."

"Lead the way," I said, grabbing my permasteel shovel.

Not far from where we started out, she stopped and pointed out a line of scrubby, twisted plants. "I think there's something underground here."

I didn't really see what had caught her attention, but that was okay. A chance of finding water was better than nothing.

The ground here was sandy, rather than the hard-pack near the base of the cliff.

"I think you're onto something," I said as I took out the first plant, continuing a narrow trench toward the next. "Look at how deep the roots are, as if they're searching for something." I dug a bit further down. "The dirt is getting darker, isn't it?"

I dipped my finger in the damp sand, sniffed it, and took a tentative lick.

"A bit of a funny taste, but I think it's safe." I shrugged. "The oddness might just be the dirt."

Yasmin pressed her lips together, then nodded. "That may be the best we get. But if it is safe, what are we going to use to collect the water in?" she muttered, eyes fixed on the ground. "Not thinking clearly, is right. I'll be right back."

Within minutes, she'd returned, hauling one of the empty oxygen tanks from her suit and a few scraps of cloth from our burrow.

She stopped next to me, panting.

"I don't think I should be running."

"No," I said flatly. "You shouldn't. The tank's a good idea, though. One of the pieces of permasteel is likely sharp enough to saw through it to open it up more." I waved at the narrow trench. "And it will fit so neatly, too."

Yasmin met my eyes. "I don't know what mods you

have, and you don't need to tell me, but I'm pretty damn sure you can rip the top right off that tank, right?"

A brilliant, resourceful woman who didn't ask awkward questions.

Void, I really hoped the previous night hadn't just been the lack of oxygen.

At the end of the hour, we'd made a crude filter out of the scraps of fabric, and a slow stream of water was trickling into our container.

"It'll take a while, but we've got other things to do," Yasmin's jaw tightened. "I've already been thinking about ways to reconfigure the communications panel into a more portable device. Shouldn't be hard, mostly a matter of managing the power supply, I bet."

I nodded. "Good, because before we drink any of that water, I'd like to be able to do better than just guess if it's safe. I want to see if there's enough of the sensors left, and how broad spectrum they were to begin with. But I'm not bringing back that AI."

The easy part would be an oxygen sensor, every ship had some version of that hard-wired in place, ready to alert to any loss of O2 in the cabin.

But surely there were enough other components that I could modify to tell if something was going to kill us before we ate or drank it.

"Let's get to work."

The scorching heat came on quickly. By midafter-noon, when we split one of the last meal packets, we didn't bother letting it heat up.

Turned out it was pretty hot anyway.

Both of our test devices theoretically were working. The communicator would let us send a message, but all it picked up was static. We had no way of knowing if the message had been received.

If anyone was even out there, looking for us.

"I think we need to get higher," Yasmin said, slumped against the cliff wall. She tilted her head back, eying the rocky heights above her.

I tore my eyes away from the delicate curve of her neck, thinking about what further modifications I could make to my sensors.

"Is it possible?" she wondered.

It should be more than possible. It should be easy to scale that cliff.

But I was getting worried.

I'd missed whatever had investigated our camp last night. And while I still felt like myself, I apparently wasn't.

Would I be enough to keep her safe?

"Sure, if we need to." I pulled up the sample of water I'd brought back from the trench. "The analyzer says the water is safe. Let's have some first, then I want to see about those plants we so ungraciously evicted from their homes. Water is not the only thing we're going to need to replace soon."

Yasmin grimaced. "They're going to taste awful, aren't they?"

"Probably," I agreed, then stiffened, jumping to my feet.

"What's wrong?"

"Don't you hear it?" I snapped.

Her look of plain confusion made it clear she didn't.

But I knew that sound, had been on too many dirt-side missions not to know it.

There was a low rumbling I could feel in my bones, a twist in my gut.

"Get away from the cliff!" I snapped. "Just head straight out!"

"What?"

"Argue with me later!"

I swung her into my arms, grabbed our prototypes, and dashed out of the shade into the middle of the desert.

"Stay here," I commanded as I put her down and shoved the devices at her. The tilt of her chin told me I was in trouble, but there was no time for explanations.

"Please."

She nodded once, and I bolted back to the cliff at top speed.

Our supplies, the scavenged components, everything except the two small devices we'd just crafted, was still at the foot of the cliff, but as I ran, I could feel the earth buck under my feet.

"Hakon!" Yasmin shouted. "Come back! It's not worth it!"

Now she knew exactly what was going on.

But we needed those supplies.

As soon as I hit the cliff face, I started grabbing everything in sight.

I glanced up to see Yasmin running towards me.

"Get back, it's not safe!" I yelled.

"Then you get out, too!" she snapped. But she stopped, backing away.

Another tremor, harder this time, as I swore up and down at myself.

Why hadn't I thought to make some sort of carry bag for all of this junk?

What was junk? What would we need?

What would make the difference between dying on this rock and survival?

Screw it.

Everything that looked like it would survive the impact I started tossing into the desert, to Yasmin's side.

But the delicate components we had so carefully harvested, that I'd planned more projects for, I couldn't go tossing about haphazardly.

We were going to lose everything.

Another quake, this time strong enough to knock me to my knees, bringing a shower of rocks down from the cliff.

It was enough, it would have to be enough.

I'd make it be enough.

Yasmin had started dragging the sheets of metal I'd thrown further away, darting forward again to grab a new one.

"Get farther back!" I shouted to her. "I'm on my way!"

But I'd waited too late.

Before I'd taken three steps, the cliff face fell down on top of me.

YASMIN

"Hakon!"

I stared at the pile of rock before me.

He couldn't be gone. He just couldn't.

Heedless of the small tremors that still rocked the desert floor beneath my feet, I raced back to what had been our little campsite.

Now, all I could see was a pile of boulders, large and small.

Our burrow and what was left of my ship were crushed.

Whatever supplies Hakon hadn't managed to fling to safety were gone, pounded to dust.

And none of that mattered.

Because he was gone, too.

I grabbed one of the scraps of metal, cursing at the burning in my lungs.

I'd never be able to dig him clear, not with the stupid lack of oxygen.

But I sure as hell could try.

I started where I'd last seen him, his eyes fixed on me as he ran toward safety.

Faster than I'd ever seen anyone run.

But not fast enough, not soon enough.

Stop thinking, Yasmin, I told myself. All you have to do is dig in.

One rock at a time.

Then another.

And another.

Using the heaviest sheet of permasteel I could lift as a lever, I shoved rocks off, rolling them down the pile to scatter on the desert floor.

But no matter how many I moved, the newly formed mountain of rocks didn't seem to go down any further.

Then I heard him.

"Little to the left, Yas."

"Seriously? You're bitching about my technique?"

Apparently having a cliff dropped on him hadn't really softened him up in the slightest.

After a grueling ten minutes, I was finally down far

enough to see his shoulder, the bare skin almost raw from the sharp stones.

I flung down my tool, touched him as gently as I could, just to be sure he was real, not a delusion caused by frantic wishing and oxygen deprivation.

"Sorry I'm not more help," he said. "I'm a little pinned right now."

"I've got it," I answered, brushing away an annoying wetness from my face. "It may take me a bit, but now that I know where you are, I can do this."

"Don't worry about me, I'll be fine."

"You impossible man," I said, but I didn't really care how impossible he was.

He was fine.

And this time I believed him.

Agonizing minutes later, I'd cleared enough space for him to be able to move, just a bit.

"I got it from here, Yas." A grunt, followed by the clattering of stones. "You may want to back up a bit, actually."

Hastily, I hurried away. I'd already caught more than a few bruises from the rocks continuing to shift and slide in the pile.

"I'm safe!" I called back to him.

"You better be," he answered, then in a small explosion of rubble, he reared up, bursting free.

And finally, I saw what the problem had been, why he'd had such difficulty getting loose.

Rather than just saving himself, he'd hunched over the last of our supplies, protecting them with his own back.

Rations, our scant, muddy water, the last salvageable electronics from my ship, all lay scattered at his feet.

I flung myself at him, scrambling over the rocks. "I'm going to kill you myself if you ever do anything like that again."

His mouth fell upon mine as if he were desperate for more than oxygen, and I pressed into his chest, anger, relief, and fear all tangled together.

Finally, I stepped back, cupping his face in my hands.

"Don't you dare tell me this is lack of oxygen," I insisted.

He pulled me back into his arms, stroking my hair while I luxuriated in the feeling that he was here. Safe. With me.

"Not going to, babe. Not right now."

After a moment, something over his shoulder caught my eye and I pulled back again. "What's that?"

A deep growl rumbled through his chest. "If it's whatever the hell made those tracks, it can come back later. I'm not in the mood for being interrupted."

"No," I said, leaning to the side so I could get a better look. "I don't think so. But you better look."

With a deep breath, he turned and for once, I saw his jaw drop.

"What the hell is that?" he barked.

The quake had opened a thin crack in the rock, revealing a narrow, twisted passageway heading deep into the cliff.

And it was glowing.

"Only one way to find out," I said, reluctantly sliding out of his arms. But this was far too interesting to ignore.

"It's glowing. The rock is glowing. That's never a good sign," he argued.

"How do we know until we go look," I asked. "Besides, what other choice do we have? We can head out into the desert, but we don't know how long that extends, and we have no idea how much water we'll be able to find." I pointed up. "Climbing the cliff isn't an option anymore. Don't even try it. You know it's not safe now, if it ever was."

Hakon scowled, but didn't say anything.

"Let's at least take a look, see what's there," I pressed on. "Right now, we can't afford to ignore any opportunities. And for all we know, right on the other side of that passage is something we need."

In the end I won, but Hakon vetoed my plan of wiggling in first for a fast reconnoiter.

"Not a chance. If we're going, we're both going."

I sighed. "How do you think you're even going to fit?"

There wasn't an ounce of fat on him, but his shoulders were easily three times the width of the opening.

"We'll make do with what we have, same as usual," was his stoic response.

He gathered all of our surviving salvaged pieces of metal, and carefully selected one, hefting it in his hands.

"I can widen the opening enough. It'll be tight, but you're not going in there without me."

"And how do you expect to avoid another avalanche?" I argued. "Banging away at that wall doesn't seem like a great idea."

"You and the supplies are safer out here this time," he reminded me. "If anything starts falling again, I'll be faster and more likely to get away."

Humph.

While he chipped away at the opening, I tried to distract myself with sorting out the components.

Far too many of them were completely fried from the crash. We'd never be able to get them to work again.

But a couple looked like they had some potential. Maybe not for their original purpose, but between the two of us, we might be able to come up with something useful.

The good ones made a small pile.

Not too much to carry, but it would be awkward without a bag of some sort. And all of our fabric was under another ton of rocks.

Glancing up at Hakon, who seemed to be making faster progress than I'd expected, I quickly unlaced my boots, unfastened the front of my coveralls, and stepped out of them.

The sudden silence caught my attention faster than another quake.

Hakon had stopped, eyes fixed on me.

"What. Do. You. Think. You're. Doing?"

"Making a bag," I answered, trying to ignore the butterflies that had just taken wing in my stomach. "If I'm careful, I should be able to reuse the top again if I need it later, but right now, this is the only fabric we have access to."

The sun beat down on my exposed skin as I stood there, just in my undershorts and tank top.

But it was nowhere as hot as his fierce gaze.

I turned away from the intensity but, drawn to him, I kept sneaking glances as I worked.

He kept watching while I cut the top of my coveralls free from the pants, cut another strip off to make a crude belt, and covered my legs back up.

Frowning at the fabric left, I refastened the front of the coveralls, then knotted the arms together to close up the neck and make a rough handle.

Carefully, I put all the components inside, wrapped in the remnants of his shirt and jacket. It would have been better if I'd had something else for padding, but I wasn't planning on giving up my pants.

When I was finished, I risked another glance at Hakon.

He was back at work on the opening, hitting the cliff face with considerably more force than he had been earlier.

"It's not great, but it'll work," I called out to him.

A grunt was the only response I got, so I kept puttering with my own project.

By the time I was finished, he was done.

"Are we leaving all the metal?" I asked.

"I'll take a few pieces with us. If nothing else, I'll feel better with some sort of weapon to hand."

"Well, that's encouraging."

He shrugged. "You want to explore a glowing cave. I want weapons. This way, we both win."

Bag slung over my shoulder, makeshift pickaxe in his hand, we stood at the opening to the passage.

"Well, at least we shouldn't need light," I said, leaning in a bit, curious about the strange glow, but unable yet to see what had caused it.

He didn't look comforted by the thought.

After a few steps, at least one mystery was solved.

Everywhere we passed, veins of some mineral glowed silvery white against the russet stone, faithfully lighting our way.

"What do you think it is?" I said, tracing it with my fingertip, fascinated by the phenomenon.

"No idea," Hakon shrugged, the play of muscles in his back drawing my attention away from the rock. "I suspect it's reacting to exposure to whatever air is down here. When we get somewhere I feel safe, I'll start testing that new analyzer."

As we continued following the twisting channel deeper into the cliff, Hakon called back over his shoulder.

"Ready to continue what we started last night?"

My cheeks burned. "I don't think we have room—" I cut myself off, realizing what he meant.

Information trade.

Right.

Time for the whole story, as much as I didn't want to relive it. "If you're new to the sector, you may not know that the corporations are almost continually at war. Some overtly, others not so much."

Hakon stopped to chisel out another bit of protruding rock that was making the crack too narrow for us.

"How far do you think this goes?" I asked, not really wanting to continue with the story.

But he wasn't that easily distracted.

"No way of telling. We'll find out when we get there, or it'll lead nowhere and we'll turn around and call it our exercise for the day."

I swallowed hard as we moved on again, the threads of light in the stone seeming to grow brighter the further we went. "Desyk Consolidated Systems and ExaTek had formed a treaty, back in my grandmother's time. Not a merger, but enough of an alliance that together we swept up scores of smaller corps, absorbed their assets, became even stronger. The partnership was working so well for everyone that we didn't consider them a threat any longer."

"That's never a good thing," was all he said. "But understandable."

"Yeah, I guess everybody was tired of fighting, willing to trust a little too much." My breath caught in my throat, remembering my father's gentle smile. He'd hated the wars between the corps. Hated conflict of any kind.

"My mom died when my brother and I were pretty young. My father threw himself into raising us and running the company with his brother. When he started dating again, we were so excited for him, and we teased him about staying out too late."

For a moment, I didn't see the walls pressing around us, didn't feel the rock under my fingers.

Just the messy living room my brother and I had taken as our domain, and Father's beaming smile as he told us about the wonderful woman he'd met.

Who he had convinced to have dinner with him.

"We thought it was past time he had a life of his own, maybe even hoped it would make things easier for us when we left to go finish our final exams. He'd have someone there with him, wouldn't be comming us constantly for our test scores."

A bitter taste filled my mouth. We'd nearly pushed him into her arms.

"But it was all a lie."

"Hold on," Hakon said softly. "It looks like we're about to find where this comes out."

Good. I didn't want to think about this anymore, anyway.

And together we stepped into a wonderland.

The cavern before us was covered with faintly glowing lines, the luminous streaks on the ceiling making a strange collection of constellations wherever they crossed.

Around softly shining stalagmites and darker hued boulders, clusters of golden and purple iridescent fungi grew, sprouting from thick beds of moss.

And strangely enough, I realized I could breathe just as easily as I ever had back on the station.

My eyes fixed on the cavern, unable to look away from each new discovery, I swung the bag off my shoulder and blindly felt for the pieced-together analyzer.

"Do me a favor? Can you test the oxygen levels here?" I handed it to Hakon. "Either we've stumbled into a pocket of air, or I'm in really bad shape and hallucinating." He growled softly, but took the device. "I'd like to know sooner rather than later."

I sat down, just in case.

Hakon scowled at me, and stomped off, muttering darkly. But he was back in moments, a clump of light blue moss clenched in his hand, the delicate tendrils seeming to wave in the air.

"You're not in trouble," he said. That wicked grin flashed again. "Or at least, not about the oxygen. If anything, it's a tiny bit higher than standard. And that's due to these little guys, I suspect."

He held the plant close to my face, and it was like a jolt of kaf hit my system.

"How is it doing that?" I asked. "Even after you uprooted it?"

"No idea, must be some sort of specialized photo-synthesis or something." He frowned at the little plant, as if by glaring he could decipher all its secrets.

"Biology shouldn't be that much different than engineering. But how living things work is just weird."

I agreed with him on that. Everything would be easier if life was more like mechanics.

Feeling better than I had since we'd crashed, hell, since I first stepped foot on Station 112, we explored the rest of the cavern.

Long hanging tendrils of pale vines wove themselves into delicate living curtains that pulled back when I brushed too close to them. Moon white flowers flickered open and closed randomly, their petals emitting a chiming sound with every movement.

As we rounded another corner, I cocked my head, puzzled. "Am I hearing water?" I asked.

Hakon nodded. "Have been for a while now."

As we wove through the maze of curtains, suddenly we found ourselves on a rocky shore.

In the silvery ambient light, the dark lake rippled like something alive, the water wide enough that I couldn't see where it ended.

"How large does a body of water have to be in order to have waves?" I wondered aloud. "We're on a moon, and as far as I know, Sat 9 doesn't have its own satellites. Apparently, there's a lot I didn't know about this place."

Hakon stood next to me, watching the lake carefully.

"No idea. But either they're waves, or something is in there, moving around. Maybe several somethings."

Huh.

I needed to think about that for a few minutes, I decided. I wandered away, feeling a little more comfortable with the glowing but completely stationary towering fungi.

When my world had been turned upside down, I'd left school and never finished the engineering degree that was all I'd ever wanted.

With a careful finger, I poked at the spongy surface of some fungi, the texture surprisingly velvety, almost soothing just to touch.

Maybe I should've studied biology instead. Maybe someday, when everything was right again, I should do that.

If that ever happened.

If we ever made it back.

"Honey," a shout from back by the lake pulled me from my spiraling thoughts. "Dinner's on!"

HAKON

I pulled the second skewer of fish off the burning moss and checked it again.

"Those things are really ugly," Yasmin said, eyes narrowed.

"True," I agreed. They were pale, rubbery looking things. No eyes that I could discern, just a strangely elongated head covered with tiny prickly scales.

But, if the analyzer was working correctly, and I was pretty sure it was, since I'd been the one to make it, eating it wouldn't kill us.

"If we're still down here tomorrow, we can start looking for other protein options," I said. "But for now, dig in."

The moss, with its excess of oxygen, had made an excellent campfire. It'd taken the slightest spark to catch, and I'd been careful to clear a wide swath of rock around it. Threading another speared fish onto a permasteel skewer, I gazed at the cavern with a combination of awe and suspicion.

"I've never seen anything like this," I admitted. "And I've seen a lot of strange stuff."

"Now you've got me curious," Yasmin said, leaning back to recline against one of those weird mushroom things. "I think it's your turn to go on with your story."

The soft light gilded her face, the plain black tank she'd worn under the coveralls highlighting every curve of her chest.

With a flash, the vision of her stripped down in the desert came back to torment me, like it had all day. The passageway that had led us here was probably wider now than strictly necessary, but chiseling into the stone had been a great way to burn off the sudden fire that had burned through me.

At least, that had been the plan. But it was still there, banked deep in my gut.

"Hakon?"

What? Oh, right.

"Like I said, we've seen a lot of weird stuff over our missions," I started. "My brothers and I are..."

I don't know why the others always made such a big deal of this.

It was engineering, plain and simple.

People would handle the knowledge of what we were, how we'd been made.

Or they wouldn't.

Either way, it didn't really affect us.

Still, for the first time, I was a little concerned as to what someone might think.

Not just someone.

Yasmin.

But I stuck to the description I'd perfected.

"My brothers and I are a Pack of illegal, lab-grown, genetically modified mercenaries," the words rolling off my tongue as quickly as possible. "At least, we *were* illegal. Recently, we've done a few favors for the new Emperor, and somehow, by the magic of legislation, we're completely legitimate now." I frowned. "Feels kinda weird, honestly."

She studied me closely. "You're not joking about any of that, are you?"

"Nope." I reached towards the campfire, my hand trembling slightly, not quite ready to meet her eyes and see the judgment waiting there. "Ready for another fish?"

"No," she said. "They're all yours."

I took one, munching through its crispy skin. They tasted just as bad as they looked. But I needed the calories.

It'd be stupid to let something as inconsequential as flavor hinder my performance.

Especially when Yasmin's safety would be on the line.

Glancing at her, the knot in my belly tightened.

Maybe I was wrong. Maybe my origins *would* make a difference to her.

"Now you've done it," she finally said. "Now I want to hear all your stories. And in all of that, you've never seen anything like this?"

I stopped chewing for a minute, pleased to know that I had been right.

The others had totally made too much of a thing about this.

Yasmin was obviously much more interested in the glowing mushroom things.

Shoulders relaxing, I studied the cavern again. "This is a new one for me. Not entirely sure how I feel about it."

"I know how I feel about it," she said, stretching her arms high above her head. "I feel fantastic. I don't think I'd realized how much I'd been struggling to breathe out there." She grimaced. "Unfortunately, it's not like we can just stay here, dining on lumpy fish and trying to figure out what makes everything glow."

"That would be terrible, wouldn't it," I said, forcing myself not to think about a quiet, domestic life with her. Maybe one that didn't involve being marooned in this bizarre cavern on an uninhabited moon.

But maybe something else.

"Solving how to get out of here can wait until tomorrow," I decided. "No idea what time it is, but we should think about setting up a camp." My jaw tightened, thinking about those tracks in the sand this morning. "I'd feel better if we had some sort of security set up."

Yasmin smiled. "I think I know just the place." Taking my hand, she led me back to the section of the cavern that had been divided up by the hanging vines into a series of small chambers.

She touched one of the vines and it made the same high-pitched tinkling sound. "Think you'd hear that, even in your sleep? Because I can hear it just fine and I know for certain your senses are sharper than mine."

I nodded, looking at the spot she'd picked out. A good-sized, relatively flat floor, surrounded by layers of the curtaining vines, some so long they pooled onto the ground. "I don't see how anything would come through without brushing against those things. Good call."

"I even have a plan for bedding," she said with a grin. "Let's see how carefully you can wield that stabbing pole of yours."

Leaving the "bedroom", we crossed the cavern. Other than the lapping water of the lake, it was eerily silent. Finally we stopped, and I stared at the giant fungus Yasmin pointed to, eyes shining happily.

I took a step back. "You want to sleep on that thing?"

"Yes," she breathed. "Just touch it." She stroked the mushroom, and suddenly, inappropriately, I felt my own shaft stiffen.

"Or at least," she continued, "I want to dissect it a bit, see if we can take the outer layers off, use it for padding like you did with the seats of my runner."

Never mind.

"I really wish I had time to make a few more sensors," I grumbled, for the twentieth time regretting every component that had been lost in the earthquake. "Everything is glowing madly, and with our luck, it's probably radioactive or something, but how do we know that?"

Yasmin turned in a circle, her arms spread wide. "If all of this is glowing due to radioactivity, sleeping on a mushroom is the least of our worries."

True.

The permasteel slid through the soft flesh of the mushroom easily, and as Yasmin carefully pulled the outer layer off, I sliced the thick membranes, unrolling it till it made something approaching a mattress.

"I haven't decided yet if this makes the list of top ten experiences," I told her as we ferried the pieces back to the vined area. "Maybe I should be keeping a list of strange things, instead of things to do again."

She stuck her tongue out at me and continued making up our mushroom bed.

I was definitely not telling my brothers about this.

I didn't even like mushrooms, even if most of the replicator stock on ships was either fungi or algae.

Mushrooms were just strange.

"I'm afraid I can't do anything about the light," Yasmin finally said, when everything was finally arranged to her satisfaction. "But I think we can manage."

Then she turned to me and wrapped her arms around my neck gently, pressing her body against mine, driving out any thoughts other than pleasure at her touch and hunger for more.

"I think it's time I let you know it wasn't anything to do with oxygen deprivation."

Her face upturned towards mine, I didn't need the low light to let me see the sparkle in her eyes, or catch the flick of her pink tongue on her full lips.

Just her touch was enough to bring that fire back into a raging inferno.

I bent my head and breathed that sweet scent in deeply. "When I saw you half naked out there in the sun, I thought I had lost my mind," I growled against her throat. "Or maybe that you were trying to make me lose it. Either way, it didn't matter."

She moaned as I nipped down the curve of her neck, teasing around the strap of her tank top.

"It wasn't on purpose," she pleaded as I plucked and rolled one tight nipple through the fabric. "At least, not much," she finally admitted.

"Did I say you weren't in trouble before?" I growled, spurred on by the idea of her wanting to tease me. "There might have to be repercussions, babe."

Capturing her mouth with mine, I ran my hands under the hem of her tank top, lightly traced my nails up her side, then swiftly pulled the thin barrier off her, leaving her bare to my eyes. "You're in all the trouble you can handle now," I promised, watching her pupils dilate and her breath start to catch.

Falling to my knees before her, I brought one nipple into my mouth, wrapping my arm around her waist to keep her close to me.

But with her moans, she made it clear she had no intention of going anywhere as her fingers knotted in my hair.

Her panting breaths turned into husky cries as I switched my attention to the other breast, dropping one hand to rub at that sweet spot between her thighs, pushing against the fabric, not surprised to feel her wetness soaking through.

"I want to do this until you scream," I said, rubbing her clit in circles, teasing it. "But I want to taste you even more."

Growling, I clawed at the stupid knot she'd tied in the stupid fabric belt holding the stupid coveralls up at her waist.

"Let me get it," she said after a breathless moment. "We don't have enough fabric if you tear this. Next time, you can shred things off me," she promised, and I couldn't tell if it was meant for me or herself.

Once the fabric was free, I pushed it down to her knees, too impatient to bother with unlacing her boots.

Fingers buried in the soft flesh of her hips, I pulled her mound towards me, lapping at her sweet nectar until she shouted, her cries echoing through the cavern.

But I wanted more.

Needed more.

Spreading her legs wider as she clutched at me for balance, I rocked her backwards until she rested on the makeshift mattress, then got rid of the boots and pants altogether.

Stripping off my own clothing, I gazed down upon her.

Glorious. Tough. Clever.

And only one word ricocheted through me.

"Mine."

He was going to drive me mad with need.

"Please," I begged, but Hakon continued his slow path up my thighs, licking and nipping until I trembled, and shattered again.

But it wasn't just his touch, nor the wicked, wonderful things he did to me with his mouth, nor the way that every move sent lightning through my body.

It was the sheer rightness of our being together. The magic that, despite everything else going on, despite the noise that was always in my head, always driving me on, I could let go.

Here, with him, nothing else mattered.

There was nothing but us.

When I recovered from being driven over the edge a

second time, I reached for his strong shoulders and pulled him up to cover me.

Resting on his elbows, his dark eyes were warm, the danger more of a temptation.

"No more teasing," I said, kissing that stern mouth that was now so sweetly irresistible. "I wasn't that bad."

The broad head of his cock nudged against my slick folds and I gasped.

"Maybe I can tempt you to be bad again," he growled as he slowly drove into me.

As we locked together, pleasures chasing each other until it was a dizzying blur of heat and need, euphoria swept through me.

Frantic for more, I kissed and bit at Hakon's neck until, with a roar, his strokes thrust even deeper, harder, until my eyes fluttered shut as frenzied nerves exploded, carrying me off to bliss with him, again and again.

I had thought that the constant light of the cavern, muted as it was, would keep me awake.

Hakon made sure I was too tired to care.

"ARE WE CALLING THIS MORNING?" I asked, sitting up bleary eyed, and looking for my clothes.

Hakon perched by the side of the makeshift bed and

gently brushed my hair out of my face. "We're the only ones down here, with no supplies and an untested comms link. I think we get to set the rules."

"Great, then I'm decreeing I want a giant cup of kaf, and something chocolate for breakfast."

"Could I interest you in some lumpy fish?" Hakon offered, and I buried my face back into the mushroom mattress.

But eventually, practicality won out. Kaf and chocolate being in short supply, lumpy fish and tepid water would have to do.

"So, what's our plan now? I asked.

"I did a little exploring this morning," he said. "It looks like there's three tunnels large enough for us to use leading out of the cavern, not counting the way we came in."

He handed me my tank top and I pulled it on, realized it was backwards, and fixed it, muttering.

"So, we have options," I said. "One," I held up a finger, "we stay here in the land of mushroom delights. Two, we go back to the desert, follow the cliff in either direction, and see if we find anything. Three, we pick a tunnel and hope it comes out someplace."

"We could try exploring the lake," he suggested. "But I don't think that's going to get us very far."

"As much as I hate to do it, I'm going to have to veto option one. This is interesting, but we can't just stay and hide here." I pulled on my pants and began to lace up my boots.

Hakon nodded. "We can always go back and visit the desert later," he said. "For now, I think we should investigate the tunnels." His eyes narrowed. "Carefully. I suspect this cavern and the tunnel system are what's left of an old river system."

I nodded thoughtfully as I re-braided my hair. "That would maybe explain the arrangement of plants in the desert."

"However, it doesn't mean we're the only ones down here. Something else could be living in those tunnels."

I stood up, grabbed the bag, and slung it over my shoulder. "Good thing you have your favorite poking stick, then."

We stuffed the bag full of the oxygen producing moss, even sacrificing a few of the components, much against my protests.

"We're not even sure half of that stuff works," Hakon insisted. "We are sure that you need to breathe."

"I suppose…" I conceded.

But he'd been right. From where the bag sat on my shoulder, the moss exuded enough oxygen that I was in a personal bubble of breathable air.

"Let's get a bit more," I decided. Luckily the cavern was full of the moss, and the fine strands wove together easily. "Bend down, just a bit?"

Hakon frowned, but complied. "Why?"

"Because you're far too tall for me to try to toss this over your head," I explained, closing the woven ring of moss around his shoulders, and adjusting the second one on myself. "If me breathing is important, it's important for you too. Don't argue."

"Humph."

"I refuse to define grumbling as arguing."

Garlanded in moss, we examined the three tunnels. One I backed out of quickly. "It smells funny," I explained. "Wrong."

Hakon tilted his head. "I can tell it smells of something, easily enough. What makes you think it's a bad something?"

Nose still wrinkled, I shook my head. "I don't know. It just makes me think of something stale, stagnant. We wanted a tunnel that leads to the outside, right? I don't think that air has moved in years."

He considered it. "Good point. Let's try the next one."

The next one didn't smell bad but, after the first few feet, the floor started to slope down.

"How far do you think it goes before it hits the water level, if we're right about that underground river system?" Hakon mused.

"I don't know." A fabulous thought struck me. "I wonder if mushrooms float?"

He glared at me. "I am not making you a damn mushroom boat." He scrubbed his face with his hands. "I can't believe I had to say that out loud."

"And the day's still so early," I chirped. Who needed kaf? There was something fabulously energizing about seeing the soft, silly side of the arrogant giant who had taken over my fabrication lab just...was that really just two days ago?

I shook my head. Time really had lost all meaning.

"Let's go try door number three."

"Well, it's technically a tunnel," I admitted, staring doubtfully at the third option. It didn't smell bad and it didn't immediately dive downward. But it was much narrower than the other two.

"Let's try the second option," I said. "This one looks a little tight."

Carefully, we made our way down the middle passage, the stone walls smooth.

"Look how smooth the walls are," I marveled. "It must have taken years and years of water flowing through here to wear away the rock like that."

"Or giant burrowing grubs," Haakon said calmly from in front of me. "If they had acid or something, they'd work through the stone pretty fast, I'd bet."

I shot his back a nasty look. "No. Water."

"Giant glowing mushrooms you're alright with, but

not grubs?" He shook his head. "That seems a little random."

The passage curved and twisted, always sloping down, until Hakon stopped, tilting his head. "I can hear the water already," he said. "We'd better turn back."

"Let's go a little further, maybe there's a way around it," I argued.

After another gentle curve, we could see another lake, like the one in the upper cavern.

The path continued across it, rising up just above the waterline to form a narrow causeway.

"See!" I said a little more brightly than I felt. "We won't even get our feet wet. No mushroom boat needed."

Hakon led the way and I followed carefully after him, casting glances at the water on each side.

"How big was the largest one of those lumpy fish that you speared?" I asked, trying to keep my voice casual while watching something dark in the water.

Several somethings.

Large somethings.

"I saw a couple about as long as my arm," Hakon answered. "Left them alone, it would have taken too much to cook them properly. Why?"

"Because those two over there seem to be significantly larger than that," I said, chest tight. "And they seem to be heading right towards us."

He spun towards where I pointed at the dark water, hunched down, spear in his hand.

Examining the water more closely, his shoulders set, fingers flexed around the weapon.

"It's not just the two you saw. There's dozens of them."

I peered around his shoulder, calculating rapidly. The narrow footpath continued across the underground lake, but I couldn't see the end of the path.

"Think we can make it to the other side?"

He looked at the path before us, then back the way we'd come. "No. Start running back," he ordered. "I'll be right behind you."

As we raced away, water sloshed over the narrow path as the giant fish approached us, making the stone slippery. I stumbled once and caught myself, palms smarting and torn.

Hakon's steps pounded behind me. "Keep running, Yas. Don't look back."

"Why not?" I shouted, but pulling on reserves I didn't know I had, pushed to move even faster, eyes focused on the slender trail of safety leading back to the shore.

Far too quickly, I had my answer.

A massive ghostly white missile launched itself out of the water. I ducked, unable to stop, and it landed on the path between us.

"Keep going!" Hakon shouted, but my feet refused to obey.

I stopped, knowing I couldn't leave him, unable to think of what to do to help.

I shouldn't have worried.

Using the spear for leverage, Hakon jammed it into the side of the monstrosity and vaulted over its body, pulling the permasteel shaft out with a sickening wet sound as he landed.

"I told you to keep moving," he said as he came up to me. Without pausing, he scooped me up into his arms, the spear pressing against my side.

"I'm sorry!" I said. "Put me down!"

"Not until we're back into the nice safe cavern with the glowing mushrooms and weird vines," he said.

Halfway up the passage, I tried again. "Unless those things can spontaneously evolve legs, we're safe."

He slowed, slightly, but didn't answer.

With a sigh, I tried my weapon of last resort. "Hakon, the spear is hurting my ribs."

Immediately he froze, lowering me to the tunnel floor while the spear fell with a clatter. "Why didn't you say anything sooner?" he scolded while pulling my tank top up to check for permanent damage.

"Because I was scared, too," I admitted. "And it really wasn't that bad. You just weren't listening."

"Humph."

At the end of the tunnel we paused, looking over the cavern. "Maybe we should stay here a few more days, see if we can smoke some lumpy fish for travel supplies," he suggested.

"You just want to stab things." I poked his side. "If door number three doesn't lead us out, we can turn around and come back. Or maybe we'll be lucky and there will be stabbing options no matter where we go."

For some reason, he didn't answer.

Before we tried the next tunnel, we made a little detour to the vined area.

"Are we declaring the day is over?" Hakon's eyebrows rose, eyes raking my body. "I'm good with that."

My cheeks burned. "Remarkably tempting, but no. I think you need a better way to carry your poking stick, in case you need both hands again."

He considered it for a moment, then nodded, pulling on one of the vines to test its strength. "Some rope wouldn't be a bad idea either."

I got to braiding while he made and tested a sling, adjusting it until he was happy.

"Ready to try again," he asked. "Or should we head back to the desert?"

"Let's try door number three." I wrapped the coil of rope across my torso. It was bulky and not terribly comfortable, and I wriggled, trying to make it work.

"A scrap metal spear and rope from vines," I muttered. "What a couple of engineers we're turning out to be."

The third tunnel turned out to be not as tight as I'd first feared. It didn't curve down, but didn't look like it was going up anytime soon, either.

"I guess we'll just see where it goes," I said. My mind spun with the possibilities. More angry giant fish? Something wonderful and strange? Or some other monster I hadn't even imagined?

"Tell me what happened to your father," Hakon said softly from in front.

And all of my worries of the future were swept away by the gut-wrenching feeling that attacked me every time I thought about the past.

"The wonderful woman he thought he might marry turned out to be a spy for Desyk," I spat. "It sounds so simple, doesn't take that many words to say, but it changed everything."

The tunnel was wider now, the ceiling a bit higher, though stalactites dotted the ceiling, occasionally reaching nearly to the ground. Hakon held back for a moment until I reached his side. He didn't say anything, just wrapped my hand with his, and we walked on, together, the path weaving through the shining columns.

"Our company had been developing a new process

for harvesting water out of the asteroid belts around Spectra 8," I explained, the words strangely dry and empty in my ears, as if all the emotion had already been wrung from them. "It was my father's brainchild, a project he spent almost as much time on as he did with my brother and me."

Silence wrapped our steps as I let myself remember, go back to how it had all gone wrong. I'd kept myself safe and warm by living in the rage, the need for revenge.

Remembering why revenge had become important hurt too much.

"She took all the files for that project, and everything else we had. Details of negotiations we'd opened with other corps were splashed all over the darknet. No one trusted our security, no one would do business with us, contracts were canceled left and right."

I stared blindly into the dimly lit tunnel ahead. "And my father knew it was his fault, all of it. My brother and I were at school when it happened, he and my uncle tried to keep the news from us, but it was everywhere, impossible to ignore." My throat tightened too much to push the words out for a moment. "He sent us a note, but he must have known it wouldn't reach our commtabs until it was too late."

Hakon squeezed my hand gently, but didn't say

anything, didn't offer useless words of comfort. He was just there.

"We found him, in the house we'd grown up in, where all of our best memories were made. Afterwards… Uncle Ran stepped in and took us in. He's spent the last ten years trying to replace the company's fortunes, to rebuild all the bridges that were burned by that one Desyk Consolidated spy."

The familiar warmth of anger wrapped around me. "And then a year ago, we heard Desyk had a secret of their own. And I decided I would go and get it."

HAKON

Yasmin's lips were twisted in a bitter smile, but I wondered if she'd even noticed the tears that marked her cheeks.

"In the beginning, it was just the usual rumors, little mentions in reports about other corps. Or an odd note in a captain's log running through that sector. It all added up to something hidden, something important, on Station 112."

She stopped, pulled back to the here and now by the pile of rubble blocking the tunnel. "Damn."

"Looks like the quake did some damage." Part of the tunnel's ceiling had fallen in, the columns of stone that had dotted our path broken and collapsed. Carefully, I edged around the pile. "I think we can get through here."

Yasmin didn't answer, too busy studying a chunk of rock, still softly glowing. "Maybe we should have figured out how to make a bigger bag," she mused. "I'd really love to bring some of this back, study it better."

"Keep your pants on," I growled. "You're distracting enough as it is."

Wrapping a short length of braided rope around her selected pieces, I slung them next to the scrap of metal she'd dubbed a spear, and together, we picked our way around the cave-in.

She glanced up at the ceiling. "Wonder how thick the rock is between us and the surface?"

"Not close enough to try to dig through unless that's our only option," I said firmly.

The tunnel kept winding, but now I was certain there was a slight uphill grade. Possibly promising, but I didn't want to get her hopes up only to have them dashed again.

Without prompting, she continued, voice steadier now. "I had a hacker friend of mine get into Desyk's books, show me their budgets. One thing I know about corps - the money will always tell you where the secrets are. For a minor fabrication station in the middle of nowhere, they're pumping a lot of money into 112."

She stopped to look at a cluster of mushrooms sprouted in a niche, prodding at them, but apparently decided against collecting more samples.

"I had two options, try to get into their headquarters, or try to pick up some clues on the other end. I'd never taken a contract before, so I wasn't really in the databases. My friend was able to show me a few tricks, nothing fancy, but enough to get into their systems, start to find my way around when I was off shift."

"What was the secret?" I asked. "What was worth all of this?"

She shook her head, face pinched into a scowl. "I don't know. It's been driving me crazy. Just before we escaped from the observation dome, I'd found a cache of hidden documents." She patted the pocket on the leg of her coveralls absently. "I only had time to copy them, not to read them. But once I get them back to Uncle Ran, it'll all be worth it."

I thought about the old man and the young one on the deck of the ship leading the flotilla that had attacked Station 112. "That was your uncle and brother, wasn't it?" I said

She looked up, cheeks coloring slightly as she bit her lip. "I should've told you sooner. I guess I got out of the habit of trusting anyone."

I waved it away. "Maybe, but we both had secrets, and I'm worried about something else. If they knew you were on the station trying to get the data, why would they have opened fire like that without knowing you were safe first?"

She folded her arms around her waist tightly. "I don't know. I've gone over it and over it, and it just doesn't make any sense. Maybe they had bad intel, thought I was already off-station."

"That's possible," I agreed. "Are you sure they knew you were there in the first place?"

"I sent them a message outlining my plan," she said, her tone a bit defensive.

"You didn't tell them in person? Messages—" I caught myself, thinking of the last time she'd received a message too late.

But she didn't seem to have heard me.

"There's no way they would've let me go," she laughed shortly. "My uncle never had his own children and has always been very protective of us. If he had his way, he'd have his 'negotiation specialists' with me at all times, making sure nothing ever dared to bump into me."

Her smile softened. "And my brother," she shrugged. "I guess you and your brothers aren't all exactly twins, but trust me, having a twin brother who is all of a minute older can make a girl's life difficult."

Silently, I took questioning her brother about his lack of concern for his sister's welfare off my mental checklist.

For now.

"The only way I was going to get to Station 112 and

find out what was going on was to go on my own. My brother couldn't have done the mission. He looks too much like our father and Uncle Ran. Even though we've been out of the corporate news for years, it was too much of a risk that someone would flag him." She chewed at her lower lip, fidgeted a bit with her moss necklace. "It's just so odd that they'd have arrived now, just when I had a chance to get those files."

"As it turns out, I'm pretty happy you took that chance," I admitted. "As long as you don't make a practice of pick-pocketing. Do you? Do we need to have a talk about this?"

She let out a shaky laugh just as a terrible thought struck me.

"Actually," I said slowly, not wanting to admit the possibility, but now that I knew more what was going on, I couldn't escape the facts. "My arrival might have given you the opening, but it might also have been the trigger that brought on the attack."

She froze mid-step, her face blank. "What do you mean?"

"Did your whole family know something was going on at Station 112?" I asked.

"They would have seen the same signs I did," she acknowledged. "And if they did get my message, they would have known I certainly thought there was something fishy there."

"So they would have noticed when the first official Imperial diplomatic mission to the Areitis Sector in a century showed up, right?"

Yasmin crossed her arms in front of her chest, stepped away to lean back against the tunnel wall, studying me carefully.

"Why did your ship end up there, anyway? Are you part of whatever is going on there?"

"I don't know a thing about Desyk's secrets, and I'm sure the Emperor doesn't either. We're only in the Areitis Sector because a couple of my brothers ended up on Heladae while it was shifting to new management."

And a few more of us were missing out here, but that didn't seem to be important to this puzzle.

Unless Jenke was a part of all of this.

Her eyes widened. "Everyone's been speculating what exactly happened there," she admitted. "The Empire took it over?"

"Not at all," I corrected her. "They just happened to be there when it all went down." Which was more or less true. Sort of. "Then the new management offered to make some introductions in the sector. Desyk was the first to make an invitation, that's all." I reached for her hand, hating the distance she'd put between us.

Slowly, she laced her fingers with mine.

"But why would they send you to Station 112?" she mused, as we continued down the tunnel.

"No idea." I squeezed her hand. "Vandalar just wants to check things out here. I'm sure he's looking for any opportunities he can find to get information. Maybe when we get back, you should talk to him. Maybe the best way to get ahead of Desyk would be to make a deal with the Empire yourself."

She rolled her eyes. "Because the Emperor is going to want to talk to me. Sure."

"Don't ever tell anyone I said this, but he's not that bad. And he's got a weakness for smart women."

Yasmin snorted. "That's not a weakness. That's rare intelligence. Maybe I'd want to meet him after all."

As the tunnel curved again, I considered ways to make sure she and Vandalar never met, without it getting in the way of her business.

Maybe she could just work through Thalcorr? Or maybe Loree would be a better intermediary. Loree would even put a good word in for me, I was sure.

Then every potential plot dropped out of my head as I stared at the chasm that broke the tunnel in half.

On the other side lay another cavern, filled with stone columns traced with light and more of those damned glowing mushrooms.

"Void take it!" Yasmin leaned close to the edge, peering down into the darkness. Crouching next to her,

I shook my head. Even with my enhanced vision, I couldn't tell how far down the bottom was.

Her shoulders slumped. "I guess we turn back, make another night in the cavern, and head back to the desert tomorrow."

"Maybe, maybe not," I said.

I gauged the width of the gap.

I could probably make it. I could probably make it carrying Yasmin and our supplies.

But I wasn't willing to risk her on 'probably.'

However, there was another option.

"I've got a plan, but if it goes wrong at all, we might lose our best weapon," I admitted.

"What happens if it goes right?" Yasmin asked.

"We end up on the other side. But if it goes really wrong, we plummet to the bottom. I'm not planning on that happening," I hastened to reassure her.

"We really need to work on how you introduce an idea," she said. "Let's hear it."

"It'll be faster to show you."

YASMIN

With anybody else, I would've been worried.

Hakon had proved he could do the damn near impossible more than once.

Even still, I was a little… let's call it uncertain.

"Hand me the rope?" he asked.

Unwinding the coil from my body, I handed it to him and he carefully bound one end of it three quarters up the shaft of the spear.

"That stalagmite over there," he said, pointing to a stone column in the middle of the far cavern, "looks sturdy enough to hold us."

With a massive heave, he cast the spear across the gap. It hit the target, the spear quivering as it stuck in the rock.

But it didn't hit deeply enough. One tug, and it clattered to the ground.

He hauled the spear back across with the vine, and threw again.

The second and third casts didn't make any difference.

I stopped him before he tried again. Permasteel was strong, but eventually even it would dull.

"What about those over there?" I pointed to a different area of the cavern, a little closer than what he'd been aiming for. "Can you reach that?"

There were no giant columns of stone, instead, a tangle of waist-high growths came up from the floor, looking rather like a miniature stone forest.

"Sure," Hakon said, "but there's not enough to hold onto, I don't think."

"Maybe it doesn't need to be a direct strike," I said. "Here, let's try adjusting something."

Quickly I found the stone samples I'd taken earlier from the rock fall and, with a shorter length of vine, bound both of them to the spear right above where the rope attached.

"Can you still throw it?" I said doubtfully. "Is it too awkward now?"

"Why do you insult me like that?" Hakon answered, checking the balance of the now top-heavy contraption.

"It may not need to stick into the stone," I explained. "What if it just needs to get horribly tangled up?"

"Well, the direct way didn't work," he agreed. "Let's try this."

He flung the spear and tethered stones towards the tangle of rocks and with a clatter, it hit midway.

"Perfect!"

"No celebrating yet," he said. "Let's see."

He pulled the vine back towards us and my heart sank at the grinding noise as the spear slid through the stones.

But then it stuck, caught by the makeshift bolo.

Hakon pulled the line sharply.

It held.

He heaved against it twice more. It didn't budge.

"I'll go over first and test it." he announced. "If it holds me, I'll come back for you."

"That's ridiculous," I argued. "How do you know whether the vines will hold up to being used repeatedly?" I lifted my chin and crossed my arms over my chest. "We go together, or not at all."

"You could've said that before I threw away my poking stick," Hakon grumbled.

Using the last bit of rope, we fashioned a crude harness to keep me strapped to Hakon's back, our bag of components and mosses strapped tightly against mine.

Clinging to his back, I tried to keep out of the way of his arms as he wrapped the vine around his wrist twice and gave it a final tug.

"Let's do this thing," he said, and jumped.

If I'd been terrified when I saw him leap from the airlock of Station 112, that was nothing to the terror and exhilaration I felt now when I was strapped to him, flying through the air.

We swung out over the gap, so fast it was just a blur before I squeezed my eyes shut, focusing on breathing in the spicy scent of his skin.

With a sudden jolt, we hit the far wall.

"So far, so good, Yas," Hakon said. "Now it's just climbing."

"Just, he says," I laughed. "Should I assume there's nothing I can do to help with the process?"

"Not really, unless you know any good stories to pass the time."

My mind was completely blank.

"I'll think of something later, I promise," I said weakly.

"I'll hold you to it," he said, and beneath my hands I could feel the broad muscles of his back as he slowly, deliberately, hauled us up the rope.

Faster than I thought possible, we were up and over the edge.

Arms shaking, I wiggled out of the harness and steadied myself by clutching a handy pile of rocks.

Irritatingly, Hakon didn't look winded at all.

"Do you need a break?" he asked, brow furrowed with concern.

"Don't you?" I snapped, unable to help myself.

"Not really," he said, untangling the vine, now stretched and shredded from the spear. He looked at it reluctantly. "Hopefully, we won't need it again, I don't think I'd trust it a second time. You were right."

I pulled the vine into a loose bundle and sank down onto a soft pile of moss. "It won't hold our weight anymore, but it might still have some uses." Knotting it into a haphazard net, I was grateful to have something quiet to do while catching my breath. "This way we could bring back even more samples."

I wagged a finger at his cocked eyebrow. "Don't laugh at me, you have to admit those rocks came in handy."

"I wouldn't dream of it," he said, then froze with an uncanny stillness, head turning slowly as he scanned the cavern, searching for something I couldn't see, couldn't hear.

"What is it?" I whispered, scrambling to grab all the supplies together into one bundle if we had to run, had to fight.

But unexpectedly, he relaxed, smiling broadly.

"Nothing's the matter. Grab as much moss as you can." He started pulling up clumps, handing them to me to stuff into the net bag. "Either I found the way out, or there's a forest of more than mushrooms growing down here." He put out a hand to help me up. "Moon this weird, I wouldn't be too surprised."

We crossed the cavern, Hakon's sure steps leading straight to another tunnel.

I was so excited by the idea of getting out from underground that I didn't even bother to look at the new types of fungi, thin blue stalks curving from halfway up the walls, ending in large pale purple balls.

Alright. I didn't look at them much, and didn't do more than brush against one.

It didn't take long before the new tunnel became noticeably brighter.

Almost painfully so.

"Well," I said as we rapidly retreated. "Hadn't really thought this part through."

We'd been bathed in the constant dim light of the caverns, making it easy to forget how strong the desert light had been.

There was no way of knowing what we were emerging into.

"Just move slowly, get acclimated," Hakon said. "I don't want us rushing out and realizing we're on a ledge halfway up a cliff."

Hands over my eyes, I couldn't help but laugh. "Feels like we've done something like that once today. Maybe we'll save another cliff for tomorrow."

Slowly, the blinding whiteness became bearable as our eyes adjusted.

We weren't halfway up a cliff, but rather on a broad rocky ledge halfway up a mountainside covered with a profusion of low, scraggly red and orange bushes.

Wandering closer to the edge, I could see a valley stretching out below us before rising to another range of peaks. I scanned the peak above us. "Shall we go get a better view, see what we stumbled into this time?" I asked.

Hakon bowed deeply. "After you."

As I panted my way up the steep slope, I was thankful for my mossy garland.

In the open air, it wasn't as effective as down in the cavern, but still, breathing was much easier than it had been in the desert.

"Almost there," I called back to Hakon. "And then, hopefully, we can get a signal out to my uncle."

He grinned at me as he came up and slipped the bag of components from my shoulder, changing it to his own.

"I won't say that there haven't been some good points about our little adventure," he said with a heated glance, "but I'd be happier knowing we can eventually get off this rock."

Before long we made it to the summit, one of a jagged range of peaks making up one wall that enclosed the valley below.

While I dug in the bag for the jury-rigged communicator, Hakon surveyed the land below.

"I think the cliff edge is back there," he finally said, pointing to a thin dark smudge of a line. "Glad we didn't try to cross the desert."

From this height, it was clear that the wastelands would have continued far past our resources.

"Or try to follow the cliff, see where it led," I added. Because from here, it didn't look like the cliff edge stopped, just kept going, as if a giant boot had smashed the desert down in one clean stomp.

"It's nicer over here, at least," I decided as I assembled the antenna and set the range. "But hopefully it won't matter soon."

I started with the family frequency, one that surely Uncle Ran and Luca would be monitoring.

"*Denau Runner* to *Foil*." My voice sounded strange, tight, even to me. "Please respond."

Static and more static. I adjusted the settings and tried again

Now instead of static, there was silence.

ELIN WYN

"Try it broad spectrum," Hakon suggested. "Right now, we could use a pickup from anyone."

As much as I hated to admit it, he was right. We could deal with corporate politics after we managed survival.

I opened it up to all channels. "Emergency assistance requested on Sat 9." I waited, wished we had more components to build a repeater. "Emergency assistance requested, we have crashed and are short on supplies. Anyone in the area receiving my signal, please come in."

A squeal, then in between bursts of static, a garbled noise.

"Was that someone talking?" I whirled to ask Hakon. "Did you hear it?"

He shook his head, jaw tight. "I couldn't tell, keep the channel open."

"Emergency assistance requested," I repeated, fighting to keep my voice level. Professional. Cool. Not desperate. "Please respond, we didn't catch what you said."

It was a voice; I was certain of it. But too mangled and garbled to hear what it said, let alone try to identify who had answered.

Uncle Ran?

Alcyon or Serrup?

That seemed unlikely, but we had no idea what had been happening back on Station 112.

"Dammit," I dropped my head into my hands.

All the way up the stupid mountain, I'd been so sure that my comm system would work.

Be strong enough.

Save us.

Hakon's large hands landed on my shoulders, gently rubbing. "Maybe we just need to go a little higher," he said softly, as the words and the caresses worked through my tight muscles, coaxing me to lean back against him.

I took a deep breath, rubbing my eyes. "We can take a look at the parts we've got left, see if we can do something to boost the range, up the signal."

"Last I checked, we were both pretty good at this." He gave my shoulders one last squeeze and stepped away. "The air up here is probably even thinner, though. Let's get back to the valley, look for places to set up camp and work on it down there."

My hands paused before I packed away the communicator. "Maybe, if we just wait a little more?"

"Sure thing," Hakon said, settling back down with his back against a rock. "We can wait as long as you want to, if you think it's going to make a difference."

The taste of acid boiled through me and spilled out. "Dammit, don't patronize me!" I said sharply, then bit my lip. "I'm sorry, that was uncalled for." Heat rushed to my face and my eyes burned, tears of frustration threatening to finally spill over. "I know as well as you do that if we can't get a clear signal, there's either a problem with the location or the device. Waiting isn't going to fix either of those things." I swallowed hard, then started taking apart the unit. "I'm just worried."

Hakon waited until I'd finished packing the device, then took the bag from me and wrapped his fingers around mine.

"I am, too," he admitted, and we started down the mountain.

HAKON

As we picked our way down the mountainside, my thoughts circled around one point.

I was failing her.

Those slim shoulders were carrying too much weight, too much worry.

Somehow, I needed to make that comm unit work and get us off this moon.

I had to make her know she was safe, protected, no matter what.

Suddenly Yasmin stopped, pointing across the valley. "What's that?" she said, a bit breathlessly. "It's gone now... wait, it's back!"

I couldn't tell if she was running low on oxygen again or not, but there was no mistaking the excitement in her voice.

Snapping out of my mental spiral, I looked where she pointed and caught it. The setting sun had caught something on the far mountainside, something that blinked and glittered in the light.

"That's gotta be some kind of metal or plexi," she said. "In everything we've seen here, have you seen anything that looked like that?" Yasmin's face was transformed, all of her disappointment swept away with this new spark of hope. "We've got to go see what it is!"

She hurried down the hill and I lengthened my stride to catch up with her.

"We aren't going to make it before nightfall," I said reluctantly, hating to do anything to dim that light in her eyes. I studied the surrounding peaks, making sure I would be able to orient myself in the morning. "Let's spend what light we have left making a secure camp, and we'll head out to find it first thing in the morning."

"Secure camp. We can do that," she answered.

Once we surveyed the possibilities, however, another difficulty arose.

"I can dig another burrow, but there's no handy wreckage to pull over us," I offered. "And the trees here are too shrubby to climb."

"Maybe we should retreat to the cave for the night?" Yasmin said. "The cavern on this side of the gap didn't have any of those vines that I noticed, but we could probably rig something up."

I considered it. "I could probably pull down enough rocks to block the entrance from inside."

"We do have another option," Yasmin said. "We press on. How long do you think it would take us to get to whatever it was that was reflecting?"

I calculated, gave up, and made a wild guess. "A few hours, maybe more. We haven't spent enough time on the surface of this moon to know how quickly darkness will fall, but being in a valley won't help."

"It's either we stay up all night looking for threats," Yasmin argued, "or we stay up all night walking to something that might help us. I know which one I'd rather do."

She was right. There was no way to find a defensible position here.

We had to move on.

After the first hour, the chill in the air grew pronounced.

"Let's switch everything into the net bag," I suggested, "and at least get your top back on you."

She nodded, her arms wrapped tightly around her waist against the cold.

Once I'd condensed everything into the net bag, it bulged at the sides a bit, but the moss kept the components in.

Hands shaking, she untied the sleeves and transformed the cut-off top of her coveralls from a bag back into a shirt.

"Aren't you freezing?" she asked as she fastened it up tightly.

"Nope." I slung the bag over my shoulders, looking around for anything else that might serve as another layer for her.

Nothing.

"Let's keep walking, at least it's a little warmer that way."

With the sun fully down, the only light was reflected from the swirling pastels of the gas giant above.

It was nowhere near as bright as the harsh daylight, but really only a little darker than it had been in the caverns. It was easy enough for me to keep one eye on the target ridgeline.

"Are you sure we're headed the right way?" Yas asked after she stumbled over the second scraggly bush in an hour.

"Yes," I said, then gave in to my instincts. "You're not gonna like this, but I promise it's not patronizing you. It's playing to our strengths."

She turned her exhausted face to me, her forehead lined with confusion. "I have no idea what you're talking about."

"I know, babe," I said, then scooped her up in my

arms and held her snuggly to my chest. "Yas, why didn't you tell me you were so cold? We should have stopped hours ago."

"What were you going to do about it?" she protested. "We just need to keep going. Find that thing, whatever it was."

"You need to sleep," I said. "I'll keep us going."

"That's ridiculous," she mumbled. "You're a ridiculous, impossible man."

"I know," I answered, even though I doubted she could hear me anymore. "Apparently, I'm pretty good at that. Don't tell anyone else, though."

Once she was sound asleep, I picked up the pace, hyperconscious of the fragile bundle in my arms.

Impossible calculations ran through my mind.

If I ran full speed, would I burn too much oxygen, cripple myself if we needed to fight?

The faster I got us to whatever the shining thing had been, would it mean we were safe?

Or had we built a fantasy based on lack of options and desperation?

Yasmin turned her face into my chest, rubbing her cheek against my skin in her sleep.

And suddenly, nothing else mattered.

I *would* get her there, keep her safe, get her off this damn moon.

All I had to do was figure out how.

The first rays of dawn touched the ridge of the mountain when I saw it.

"Yas, honey," I whispered into the top of her hair. "I think you're gonna want to see this."

She made adorable noises, and I reconsidered waking her up.

How many more quiet moments like this would we be able to have?

Except, really, she'd want to see this.

"Wake up, babe." I squeezed her closer to me. "I think we found our ride out of here."

Her eyelids flew open. "What do you mean? How is it light out?" She kicked her legs, scrambling to be let down. "Have you been walking, carrying me all night?"

Lowering her legs to the ground, I let her slide down my body, still keeping her trapped in the circle of my arms. "Considering we weren't in a safe enough area to do any of the other things that I'd rather do to you, that seemed the better option."

I was never going to stop teasing her if her cheeks flushed like that every time.

"You must be exhausted," she pushed away, chin high. "We should find a place to rest and—" She stopped mid-sentence. "Did you say a ride out of here?"

Gently taking her by the shoulders, I turned her until she faced what had caught yesterday's failing light, signaling us from across the valley.

"What is a ship doing here?"

"I'm guessing they crashed, same as us. But unlike us, they managed to avoid running into a cliff."

She walked towards the blocky gray craft, slowly, considering. "I haven't seen a model like this in years. You?"

I shook my head. "Not from here, remember? The ship design isn't anything I'm familiar with offhand, other than I'd guess it was meant for practicality rather than comfort." I walked around the craft, checking it over. "But I'll bet there's enough of it left we can get her up and running."

On closer examination, the damage appeared to be fairly minimal. "Except for that one buckled landing strut, you'd almost think they'd landed here on purpose, instead of crashing."

The rest of the struts had sunk into the soil, and fallen leaves and branches covered most of the ship's body. I pulled them off carefully, revealing the scorch marks of an atmospheric entry.

"The panels under the nose took some damage when they hit," Yasmin added, crawling out from underneath the frame. "We won't be able to tell how severe it is until we get inside." She brushed leaves from her hair, frowning. "But why is it here?"

"Only one way to find out," I answered, moving

towards the entry hatch midway down the body of the ship. It was open, just a crack.

Never a good sign.

Yasmin stepped toward the hatch, but I held her back. "We've got no idea who's in there," I explained. "Or what's taken up residence in the years since this crash."

"Hopefully not a cousin of the ugly fish," she agreed.

I readied my spear and motioned for her to stay close behind me, then we went up the short flight of stairs, squeezed through the opening, and paused, waiting, listening.

After a short entryway, the hatch opened to a narrow corridor running the length of the ship. To the right would be the cockpit, to the left would likely be crew quarters, maybe a cargo bay.

The ship design might not be totally familiar, but really, there were only so many ways to box together all the functions humans needed to survive the Void.

Traces of old muddy tracks covered the deck, overlapping too much to make out what they were. "Something's been up and down, all over this thing," Yasmin whispered.

Deep claw marks scored the cabinets set into the bulkheads, but none of the panels appeared to have been opened.

"Depending how long it's been here, the supplies might still be good," I murmured, still mentally circling through what it would take to get this hunk back in the air again.

Straining my hearing to the limit, I heard nothing but the wind through the bushes outside. The interior of the ship was silent, musty.

"Which way?" Yasmin asked.

"Doesn't matter, I don't think." I took another sniff. Nothing. "I don't think anyone is in here."

If you ignored the faded muddy prints that seemed to cover everything, the cockpit looked intact, as if the pilot and crew had just walked out.

Yasmin ran her fingers over the controls. "If the engines work, I can fly this thing," she said. "It's a bit out of date, but not too bad."

"That's a plus," I said. "Now let's see if we can find the engines."

Slowly, we made our way aft.

A cramped galley.

Cargo bay.

Crew quarters. All empty.

But finally, rifling through one of the two minuscule crew rooms, Yasmin found something.

A thin sheet of plexi with a circular logo of some type on it, had slid behind the door.

"Desyk," she said, tapping it, jaw tight, voice flat.

"What were they doing here? And if this was an official corporate mission, why is this the only indicator?"

"Maybe scouting for resources?" I offered. "If they could resupply the station from down here, wouldn't that save them money?"

"Maybe..." Yasmin traced the logo with her fingertip. "But now I'm even more curious as to what happened here."

"Some mysteries we may not be able to solve." I put my hand on her shoulder, rubbed the tightly knotted muscles. "Right now, we need to focus on seeing if we can get this back in the air. Or at least see if they've got supplies or even an oxygen generator."

Yasmin perked up at the thought of tangible tasks rather than more questions without answers. There'd be plenty of time for those once we'd sorted out survival.

"Engines first," she said decisively. "If I'm remembering right, they should be this way."

A bit further aft, she stopped mid-corridor, crouched, then started pulling up panels set flush into the deck.

"Ta da!" she exclaimed, eyes sparkling. "Hold my ankles, will you?"

Before I could argue, she'd lowered her torso into the undercarriage, hanging upside down, leaving only her legs and ass visible as she continued her report.

"Surprisingly, everything looks like it's in good shape. Maybe a few switches were blown during the descent, and everything will need to be recalibrated, but it looks workable."

Holding her slim ankles to keep her secured, the words flowed over me as I admired the view.

Even hidden in coveralls that were uglier than lumpy fish, the curve of her hips was mesmerizing, completely—

"Did you hear anything I said?" Yasmin popped out of the compartment, the corners of her lips curved into a bewitching smile.

"Actually, something else was on my mind," I admitted.

"I could tell," she said, one eyebrow cocked. "I think I've restored power to the majority of the ship systems. Let's see if we can get that hatch closed and secured."

Now that I'd regained a little focus, I could hear the soft, high-pitched whine as the ship came back online and proceeded to run through its internal checks.

Then the faintest hiss began.

"The internal atmosphere generator is still functional?"

Yasmin nodded. "I mentioned it. You were distracted."

I took a deep breath, not thrilled by the musty air that rushed through my lungs, but happy to know that the ship's air scrubbers would clean it shortly. Best of all, it would pump in the correct balance of oxygen and give us one safe space for the simple act of breathing.

"How long can this run?" Even if the ship was structurally sound, even if the engines only needed calibration, it would be at least a day or two before we could trust it for space flight.

If we could even get it off the ground.

Halfway back to the entry hatch, Yasmin stopped, tapping at one of the clawed closures until it opened, revealing a fully stocked supply cabinet.

"That's the strange thing," she said. "The engines have enough life to go for a month or two until they need to be recharged. The inventory logs show the ship as fully stocked." She ran a hand down the stack of rations. "I thought maybe it was an error, but apparently not."

Curious, we checked the rest of the cabinets as we went. More rations, and not just emergency packets. Replicator stock. Water cubes.

It was all still here.

With the power restored and the track cleaned of debris, the hatch slid easily back into place, sealing us in.

"What if the crew is still out there?" I hadn't seen any human tracks leading away from the ship, but it was possible. "They'd know the code to get in."

Yasmin grinned. "Not anymore. If they want in, they'll have to knock."

Wrapping my arms around her, I kissed her, unable to resist having just a taste of her sweetness. "Clever lady." After a bit, I reluctantly pulled away. "Al-right, I suppose we need to get to work."

She shook her head. "I have a better plan." She stroked the outer curve of my ear, and my knees might have gone just a little weak.

Maybe.

"You're going to get some rest, and I'm going to see what the problem is with these engines," she continued.

"Not happening," I said flatly, knees firmly back under control.

"Do you think there's anyone left on this ship except for you and me?" she asked, voice suspiciously sweet.

"No, but that doesn't mean there isn't anyone around," I insisted. "Or whatever made those tracks."

"So, as long as I work inside the ship, and keep the hatch sealed and coded, I should be safe?" that honey sweet voice pressed on.

"Probably," I admitted grudgingly.

"That's easy enough," she said. "I want to dig around in the logs, check the system's readings, figure out what happened here." She wiggled her eyebrows. "Maybe even find a proper tool set."

Her grin spread and she went up on her tiptoes to

ELIN WYN

wrap her arms over my shoulders. "And if you're very good and don't argue, I promise to wake you up in interesting, exciting ways."

Dammit.

I was never going to win an argument with her with that sort of leverage.

YASMIN

Who would have thought that after sleeping in a trench and a cave, my giant would put his foot down about clean sheets?

"If we can't find clean ones, I'll just sleep on the cot." He started rummaging through the supply cabinets. "Or use an emergency blanket."

"Really?" My brain boggled, just a bit.

Despite the lines of exhaustion carved into his face, his gaze didn't allow for any argument. "Really. Those things stink."

Right, then.

"I'll go pull the inventory logs, see what I can find."

Not the first thing on my to-do list for the ship, but if it meant he'd get some rest, it was worth it.

New sheets found, and the bed remade surprisingly neatly, Hakon still stalled.

"Repairs will go faster if we're both working on them," he insisted.

"It'll go faster if you stop arguing, go to sleep, and let me get started," I said, hands on his chest gently pushing him backwards until the backs of his knees hit the edge of the mattress.

He sank down and I knelt to unlace his boots.

Halfway through the first one I realized he'd stopped moving entirely.

I glanced up to see his dark eyes fixed on me, heat overruling exhaustion.

"None of that until you've slept." I held a finger up quickly. "A full shift of sleep," I clarified.

"I don't need that much downtime," he grumbled, but stopped fussing.

Pulling the sheets over him, I was tempted to give in for just a moment.

Curl up next to him even if we did nothing more than snuggle.

The voice in my head snorted.

Snuggle?

When did snuggling become so high on my list of things to do?

Reminded of my actual list, I kissed him on the forehead and went back to the engines.

Now that I'd had an initial look at the engine compartment, I could see where I needed to go to get more comfortable and right-side-up access.

After the first hour of work, nothing was any clearer.

The engines were fine. Nothing that would be winning any interstellar races anytime soon, but solid and functional.

I hauled myself out, went back to the cockpit, and flicked the comms system on.

This time I skipped the family channel and went straight to the widest broadcast band possible.

"Emergency assistance requested," I repeated. "We have crashed on Sat 9 and need assistance."

Nothing but static.

The atmosphere might be thin, but something was interfering with communications.

Right. On to the next task.

"Systems engage, replay last ten log entries."

Nothing answered me.

Either there was no AI, it had been damaged, or it only responded to authorized voiceprints.

No matter, I could work around that.

Thankful once again for my friend's tutorial in getting around basic computer security protocols, I got to work.

Even if I hadn't found that bit of plexi with the

Desyk logo on it, once I was in their systems, it was obvious.

Status reports and log files, all using the corporation's internal filing structure that I'd become so familiar with back on Station 112.

And all of them date-time-stamped ten years ago.

Hours passed as I read, going back in time, searching for answers.

Naval and Hill had been the crew assigned to the ship.

They'd been a resource discovery team for a number of years before their final trip to Sat 9.

As far as I could tell, their method was the same as similar teams that ExaTek worked with.

The Areitis Sector was huge. There was simply no possible way any one corporation could explore all of it thoroughly.

Resource discovery teams were sent out, hopping from one promising location to another as quickly as possible.

They were seldom staffed with environmental experts or scientists, rather with pilots who didn't mind the long hours in exchange for no one looking over their shoulders and plenty of privacy.

Teams took sample readings and sent everything off to home base, where massive AIs sorted, analyzed, and flagged the most promising discoveries for further review.

But what had they been doing here?

The moss that exuded an excess of oxygen was interesting, but hardly groundbreaking. I'd bring back the samples we'd collected, just in case, but Naval and Hill hadn't reported anything like that.

Granted, I'd been asleep for most of our trek across the valley, but surely Hakon would have mentioned if he'd seen anything unusual.

My brain caught on the word.

Unusual.

How unusual was it that he'd been able to carry me throughout the entire night without stopping?

Unusual.

Inhuman.

With everything that had been happening, I hadn't had a chance to really think about what he'd told me back in the cavern.

How had he phrased it?

A Pack of illegal, lab-grown, genetically modified mercenaries.

Leaning back in the pilot's seat, I weighed each word in my mind and set it against what I knew of Hakon.

Bigger, faster, stronger than anyone I'd ever met.

Smarter and kinder, as well.

I could only hope that the rest of his brothers, his Pack, had the same temperament.

But they weren't my concern.

The beep of another completed search brought my attention back to the logs.

Naval and Hill had only been here two days before their reports stopped.

No transmissions. No changes to the inventory. No further use of power.

With their engines and most of the structure of the ship in good shape, why hadn't they left?

Most importantly, where were Naval and Hill now?

The final log entry had no more urgency than the previous.

Despite a hard landing, no problems. We'll radio for pickup if needed, but Naval doesn't expect any issues.

Hill's voice was calm, almost bored.

I guess if your entire life was bouncing from one uninhabited planetoid to the next, it took a lot for you to get enthusiastic.

But after that, there was nothing.

Drumming my fingers on the control panel, I realized it had been hours since Hakon had agreed to rest.

Which meant I should go find out what the food situation was really like.

There was a replicator in the tiny galley. Despite the online lights, I eyed it doubtfully.

If it hadn't been cleaned or serviced in ten years, it might be better to go with the rations. Fewer options, but less chance of getting sick.

Prudence won out over taste buds.

I grabbed a random stack of bars and a couple of squeezeboxes of water and returned to the engine compartment.

"There's nothing wrong here," I muttered. "Maybe I'm not seeing it. Time to try something else."

Back in the cockpit, I finished my meal while starting a series of pressurization tests. Engines wouldn't do us a bit of good if the hull wasn't completely sound.

"And I think that's it."

There wasn't anything else I could do for now, other than worry.

Brain full of information but no answers, I drifted back to the crew room we'd taken over.

Hakon sat up quickly, eyes sharp and demanding as I slid open the door.

"What's wrong?" he snapped.

"Nothing," I said, unlacing my boots. "But now you've spoiled my surprise. Go back to sleep."

I stripped down to my underpants and tank top and slipped into the circle of his outstretched arms.

"I can't wake you up in interesting ways if you're not sleeping," I teased, snuggling into his chest, reveling in the warmth of his body, the strength of him.

How he made me feel safe.

Maybe even... stop it, Yas. No reason to go there.

"I *was* sleeping," he protested, running his hands down my spine, stopping just before the curve of my ass, kneading the tight muscles of my hips that I hadn't even noticed when I was working in the engine compartment. "Until you woke me up."

"But you're not sleeping now," I argued, rolling onto my side. He lifted me until I lay on top of him, stretched down his length.

Well, at least as far as I could stretch, given our height difference.

"So, if I was still sleeping," he said, "what would you have done?"

And now I was on the spot.

Pushing myself up to kneel across his chest, I covered his eyes. Obediently, he left his eyes closed as I removed my hands.

"If you were sleeping," I said, "I might begin like this."

Softly, I dropped featherlight kisses at the corners of his eyes, alternating down his cheekbones, back up along the outer edge of his ears, which I just now noticed were ever so slightly pointed.

His hands tightened around my calves where I knelt across him, but he made no sound.

"Or maybe I might do something like this."

Lightly, I ran my nails through the heavy stubble that covered his jawline.

He let out a low moan, a rumble that echoed through his chest. "If you kept up with that, I wouldn't be sleeping long."

His hands stroked my calves and moved up to my thighs, seeking, exploring, never resting.

Leaning over, I nipped down the cords of his throat to his collarbone.

"Pity you're such a light sleeper."

"I wouldn't want to miss any of this," he said. "You can wake me up anytime."

Though his hands slid up and down my legs, fingers sending bolts of lightning through my nerves, he seemed content to let me play.

"We might regret this later, but I can't argue with you losing your jacket and shirt in the crash," I admitted. "It's given me plenty of ogling opportunities the last few days."

"Really," he grunted. "I'll try to keep that in mind for the future."

I froze for a second, distracted from kissing down the curve of his shoulder.

Keep in mind?

For the future?

Did we, *could* we have such a thing?

Too many questions.

I shoved them all to the back of my mind and focused on here and now.

Because now was pretty damn good.

Squirming down his torso, I kept kissing a trail downward until Hakon's hands clamped around my waist.

"I think I'm awake now," he growled, and in one swift motion rolled over, pinning me beneath him.

Then his eyes flew open. "Why the hell are you still wearing any clothing?"

HAKON

Clothing swiftly dealt with, I returned my attention to where it belonged.

Yasmin.

"Even when we're just walking, I can feel you under my hands," I murmured as I kneaded one breast, rolling the rosy pebbled nipple between my thumb and forefinger. "Your silken skin at my fingers."

As if desperate to wring every bit of sweetness from her, I plundered her mouth with my tongue.

Yasmin groaned wordlessly, body arching beneath my touch.

"I can always taste you," I nipped at that sweet intersection of her neck and shoulder, worked down to take her tight bud into my mouth.

"Hakon, stop teasing," she moaned as I slid further

down, tracing the line of her hip, the delicate fold where her leg met her body.

"You're always in my thoughts now." Sliding my fingers through her slick folds, I paused for a minute, sucking and nibbling at her clit, savoring the moment, how she lay open and willing before me, then I plunged a finger into her tight channel.

Yasmin shrieked, heels drumming against my back. I drove on, pushing her closer to the edge until she went rigid, shuddering, coming undone in my arms.

Crawling back up over her chest, I propped myself up on my elbows as I brushed dark strands of hair from her softened face, watching her eyes regain focus.

"Listening to you come undone only makes me want you more," I said, nudging the straining bulk of my cock against her swollen mound.

She trembled under me, her pink tongue darting out to lick her lips. Placing her feet flat, she lifted her hips, just enough to rub against my cock.

"That's good," she purred as her arms twined around my neck, pulling me down to her. "I wouldn't want it any other way."

She rocked against me again and any control I had was lost, shattered against my need to have her, claim her. Sinking into her wet heat, I groaned when she tightened around me.

Mad with need and desire, I rammed into her until

we both roared our release, falling tangled into the sheets.

With the last of my strength, I managed to roll over, carrying her with me so she lay draped across my chest, panting.

Even with the fresh sheets, the room had still held the faint ghost of its former occupant, a trace of his scent.

But not anymore.

The very air was full of Yasmin.

Of us.

And I liked it that way.

"Waking you up is going to be an exhausting prospect," she said, chuckling softly.

"Only because you're so tempting." For a moment, I thought she'd fallen asleep, relaxed and drowsy.

But then she sat up, brushed her hair back, and began to braid it back away from her face.

"The pressurization check should be done by now," she said. "Want to come see if I'm missing anything?"

Not really, I thought to myself. Not in the slightest.

Even if it was the practical thing to do.

"You're a competent engineer," I said as I searched for my clothing among the bedding that somehow had ended up all over the floor.

"Just competent?" Yasmin shot back, throwing her braid back over her shoulder.

I tossed her coverall top at her. "There's not a good answer to that, is there?"

"Probably not." Then lines of worry marred her forehead. "I just can't figure it out. If there's something wrong with the engines, I'm not seeing it. And if there's not, then why is this ship still here?" She shrugged into the top. "I don't want us to solve that particular mystery when we're halfway back to Station 112 and something blows."

Stepping into the corridor, we headed back to that cramped engine compartment. "After this, we can check atmospheric pressure, see if we're space worthy. And then, fire up those engines."

Yasmin pulled the hatch up for the engine compartment and I shook my head. "There is no way I'm fitting down there."

She looked at me, looked at the compartment.

Blinked.

"Right."

Together we removed more of the deck until I was able to awkwardly crouch in the tight little space. "I'd like to have a word with whoever designed this ship's configuration," I grumbled.

"I'm sure they weren't expecting you to come visiting."

But all the hassle was for nothing. "Everything looks fine to me," I said, slipping the last casing back into place. "Let's put the floor back together and check the readings from the front."

They looked fine, too.

And atmosphere had held, as well.

"Looks like we might have a possible weak spot over in section 12." I tapped the 3D model of the ship the command console had placed in the air between us to enlarge it, and spun it around. "Wouldn't be much to reinforce the area if they've got reasonable tools on board."

Yasmin nodded. "This sort of exploration vessel would almost need to have a full kit. They wouldn't usually head back home for months, maybe even years."

"Let's check that panel on the outside," I decided. "I want to see if it's one of the ones that took the scorch damage, give us an idea of what we're working with."

But when I opened the exterior hatch, a new set of priorities became urgent.

"Void."

"Are those…" Yasmin asked as she peered around my side.

"Yep. Same tracks that were around the trench back in the desert." I scanned the area, but nothing was moving. "Either there's more than one of those things, or it's followed us. And I'm not sure which of those options I like the least."

Chest tight, I darted back into the ship and grabbed the spear.

"Aren't there any other weapons on this thing?" I asked Yasmin before going back outside.

She shook her head, braid flying. "The inventory logs show that there were two heavy-grade blasters. But they're both missing."

Lovely.

I stepped out again, bent low to the ground, and sniffed one of the tracks. It smelled like sour fruit, mixed with something I couldn't place, something I'd never run into before.

"Stay inside until I check it out," I said. "I want to make sure whatever this thing is, that it's long gone."

"Hakon!" Yasmin shouted. "Watch out!"

Suddenly I was flattened, face-down on the ground.

Pushing up, I twisted at the hip, pulling my legs out to strike out with both feet to shake my opponent off me.

But it had already sprung a safe distance away, giving me time to study it, look for weaknesses.

Standing before me was a purple and blue spotted *thing*.

A long, curved neck led to a round, bulbous head.

A heavy body ended in six stubby legs. It was as tall as I was, but so dense, I thought I'd have its footprints on my back for weeks.

It bounced back-and-forth, thick tail thrashing the ground as it prepared to attack again.

I crouched, ready to launch the spear.

"Stop!" Yasmin yelled frantically. "It's friendly!"

"It's what?"

"I think it's playing with you," she continued, slowly stepping out from the ship.

"Get back to safety," I shouted, trying to keep her and the creature in view. Would it renew its onslaught if I moved between them?

But she ignored me, approaching the monster with her hands outstretched.

"You just want to say hi, don't you?" she said in a soothing voice.

It bounced on those slightly bowed legs again, head whipping towards her, then lowering to the ground and up again.

"Yes, you do," she crooned. "Such a good boy." In the same singsong voice, she said "Way back when we were kids, our father got a pair of puppies for Luca and me. Well, droids really. But they'd been programmed with all of a natural dog's characteristics and behaviors."

She took another step, reached out with her hand towards the creature.

I readied myself, forcing twitchy muscles to stay still, to let her play the game the way she wanted to.

But I would spear that snakey neck into the ground before it...

Let her rub it beneath the chin?

Huh.

"I mean they didn't look anything like this, of course," Yasmin said, continuing to scratch under the rounded head with one hand while her other hand stroked the sinuous neck. "But the bouncing, the play bows, weirdly they track pretty well."

She patted the thing's shoulder and turned to me, keeping one hand on it. "Maybe they're just one of the dominant life forms and they're all over the moon," she said. "It's hard to believe that it could've followed us through the caverns, especially over the chasm. Maybe it knew the way over the cliff, and we should have followed it?"

It head-butted her, making an odd high-pitched whistling sound as she resumed scratching it. "I think I'll call you Bobo. That was my puppy's name, way back then." Yasmin glared at me. "Stop laughing. I was five."

Another bump from Bobo, demanding her attention, set her laughing. "I think you can put the spear down now," Yasmin said.

Then a howl broke through the brush and Bobo screeched in pain as a blur of orange and green tore him away from her.

This time, there was no need for Yasmin to brief me on behavioral characteristics.

Predator and prey were perfectly clear.

The terrified shrieks of Yasmin's new friend echoed through the clearing around the ship as its attacker bit and clawed at it mercilessly.

A broad, angular head ended in a thick neck. Razor-sharp claws tipped short-fingered hands, disturbingly human-like on powerfully muscled arms.

The whole body was designed as a perfectly balanced killing machine.

Yasmin screamed, jerking me back to the here and now.

While I certainly didn't have an interest in getting involved in the evolutionary cycles of this place, she was going to be upset if that thing killed her new little friend.

And maybe it had been kinda cute, once I got over the whole stomping-on-me-to-say-hello thing.

"Over here," I shouted, waving the spear to try to get its attention.

The attacking creature ignored me, focused on killing off its next meal.

But it didn't have that luxury when I rushed up and shoved the spear between its ribs, then jerked it away, leaping back to a safe distance from those fierce claws.

Bobo lay panting in the dirt as the predator turned, snarling, to face me.

"One of those heavy-duty laser blasters would be handy about now," I muttered, shoving the butt of the spear against the largest rock I could find, readying for the monster's charge.

Faster than I would've dreamed possible, it crashed through the underbrush, lips pulled back to reveal wickedly long pointed incisors.

It tickled a memory, but there wasn't time to think about it anymore, because, with a powerful spring, it was on me.

Raising the point of the spear, I caught it mid-belly as it leaped at me, then let its own momentum carry us over, flipping in mid-air so that when we landed, it was on its back, belly up.

I stood on its chest, spearing through its heart, stabbing again and again.

Finally, it stopped fighting, dark burgundy blood pooling beneath it. Yanking the spear out, I called over my shoulder.

"Yas, are you okay?"

No answer.

I whirled about, heart in my throat, only to find her kneeling over the still purple and blue spotted form.

"Can you go get the med kit?" The words were soft,

choking out of her. "It should be in the first cabinet to the left by the hatch."

She was bloody up to the elbows, her hands desperately trying to stop the bleeding from the long gashes in Bobo's pebbly hide.

"On it." I rushed for the hatch, but my hand paused for just a moment as I reached for the kit.

Were we really going to waste medical supplies on a creature that was about to be meat anyway?

Wasn't this what natural selection was all about?

But Yasmin's voice had been desperate.

She would be heartbroken if that thing died. Which meant it was going to live, natural selection or not.

Med kit in hand, I knelt by her and cracked it open. "Let's see what we've got in here," I said softly as Bobo made soft whistles and clicks.

If I didn't know better, I'd almost think the damn thing was talking back to her.

As Yas moved her hands slowly off the wounds, it was clear that the blood had already started clotting.

"Let's just get those sealed up," I said. "You might want to watch its teeth. His teeth." Yasmin had moved out of the way, kneeling by Bobo's head. "This might sting. He might bite or thrash around from the shock."

"He's not gonna bite me," she said, tears rolling disregarded down her cheeks as she moved the giant head onto her lap. "He's just scared."

Bobo gave a trill of displeasure as I sprayed the first layer of sealant. "I know kid," I said, awkwardly rubbing an unmarked section of skin. "It's not any fun. But it's good for you."

Another spray, another trill.

And another.

And all the while, Yasmin rubbed the creature's head, scratching under its jaw, talking nonsense to it.

When I was done, we were both bloodied, but the little cries of despair had eased up, and all the wounds were closed.

"Yas, honey," I said, moving to stand next to her. "I don't know if there's any internal damage. We just don't have the tools to tell us anything useful, even if it was a critter we'd ever seen before."

"I know," she said. "We've done everything we can. If he dies, I just didn't want him to be alone."

Bobo struggled to lift his head out of her lap, his trills louder now.

And from the other side of the mountain, something answered.

Something big.

YASMIN

"No, Bobo," I cried. "Stop moving!"

Head swaying back and forth, tail thrashing, he struggled to get back to his feet.

"You're going to tear the sealant," I scolded, "then where will you be?"

"Yasmin," Hakon said softly. "Come over here, please."

"But he's going to—"

I cut off sharply as I saw Hakon's face.

Carefully still, looking at something behind me.

"What is it?" I said, half whispering, too scared to look.

"I suspect it's Bobo's mother," he answered. "And I would really appreciate it if you would slowly, without any sudden movements, come stand behind me."

A trickle of ice ran down my back.

For the first time, since we'd met, he actually sounded scared.

I wasn't entirely certain I wanted to know what could scare him.

Bobo's trills grew in intensity with every step as I made my way back to Hakon, but despite feeling as if a squad of snipers had focused on my back, I refused the urge to turn, to look and see what had gotten the creature so excited.

Hakon reached an arm out for me, wrapping it around my waist and gently lifting me the last few inches until I was snugly tucked into his side.

Then I looked.

All of the air rushed out of me in one big whoosh.

Bobo was big.

Probably as tall as Hakon, and twice as long.

Mama, if it was the mama, was twenty times the size.

Everything that had made Bobo cute, big black eyes, oversized head, little bumpy baby horns, was terrifying when it was twenty times larger.

The giant purple head swooped down, almost as big as Bobo's entire body.

Three horns curved out of the skull, ending in menacing points.

With a huff that I could feel from yards away, the mother sniffed over Bobo, nuzzling at his neck.

Bobo trilled at the giant, who only rumbled in response.

Finally, apparently satisfied, the beast picked up Bobo in her mouth, turned away, and passed out of our vision around the crest of the mountain.

I sat down quickly, my legs no longer able to hold my weight, even half leaning against Hakon.

He shook his head slowly, watching where they'd gone.

"I was not ready to fight that thing," he finally said. He glanced down at me. "Are you going to be alright without your new buddy?"

"Of course," I insisted, even though part of me had been half wondering if there was a way to coax Bobo into the ship. A small part, but it was still there. "He's with his mother and is safe. That's all that matters."

Slowly getting to my feet, I took my first look at the creature Hakon had killed.

Even knowing it was well and truly dead, it gave me the shivers.

"Like some sort of a cross between a dinosaur and a sabretooth tiger," I muttered.

"That's what it was," Hakon said coming up behind me. "Something about the teeth looked familiar. When we get home, don't tell Doc that I blanked out on that, would you? She'll have me reviewing vids for weeks."

He knelt down next to the carcass. "Does that scar on its side look like blaster scorch to you?"

I looked where he pointed, reluctant to touch the thing myself.

"It could be," I admitted. "But where would it have... Naval and Hill."

Hakon nodded grimly. "I think we've found what happened to our missing crew."

"I suspect you're right." I thought about the men who had recorded those logs. There hadn't been enough in their terse reports for me to get a feeling for who they'd been. No personal mementos on the ship to give me an idea of the families they'd left behind.

But surely, there was someone. Somewhere.

Still waiting.

Hakon laced his fingers with mine. "Do you want to be sure? We can check."

"What do you mean?"

"Your Bobo might've been cute, but he stank." Hakon grimaced and pointed at the dead thing at his feet. "This one is worse. It wouldn't take too much to track it back to its lair."

I looked at the ship, thought about the list of tasks still to be done before we could safely attempt to take off.

And thought about how horrible it would've been if, ten years ago, my father had just disappeared.

Worse than what my brother and I had found when we raced home.

At least we'd had answers.

"If we can," I nodded decisively. "I'd like that."

I couldn't see the tracks, certainly couldn't smell anything, but Hakon moved through the brush without hesitation.

After about an hour, we reached an opening in a rocky hillside. "No one's home," Hakon said, sniffing the air again. "It's rank enough from years of use, but I'd smell something if it was currently occupied. Should be safe enough to go inside."

Here, I could definitely smell the scent Hakon had been tracking.

"It's like," I shook my head. "I don't even know what? What's the worst thing you've ever smelled?"

Hakon's nose was wrinkled in distaste. "No idea. Wouldn't want to remember. Let's see if we can find any proof the crew was here, and try to forget we ever smelled this."

Through the strong beam of the portable light we'd taken from the ship, I knew we'd found the right place.

A pile of bones of all sizes was pushed to the side of the cave.

And all of them were well chewed.

But a glint of metal caught my eye under the grisly tangle.

"What's that?"

Hakon kicked the pile out of the way until we found fragments of a flight suit. Maybe two. Torn and faded, the Desyk logo was still recognizable on one of the pieces.

Carefully, I gathered up every scrap of material I could find and folded them together. "Their corp and ours might be enemies, but their families deserve to know what happened to them."

Hakon rubbed my back and I leaned into his solid strength.

"Let's get out of here before we find out if the thing had a mate," he said. "I'd be plenty pissed if something happened to you. I'd expect the same from anything else."

That was sweet, but odd.

Very odd.

Thoughts tangled up in the horrible fate the resource discovery team had met, I followed Hakon back to the ship.

Once I'd stowed the scraps of fabric away, we turned back to the task at hand.

Getting off this place.

Getting home.

Well, at least back to Station 112.

Anything after that, we'd have to sort out when we got there.

"I've got the toolkit," Hakon said. "I'm going to reinforce that section, just in case. I'll let you know when I'm done, and we can start the full engines test."

Panel reinforced, engines tested, fired, and tested again.

We were ready to go.

Together, we sat in the cockpit and I began the preflight check.

"Think we're really getting out of here?" I asked.

"I'd expect so," Hakon said. "If nothing else, we'll break through enough atmosphere to try to send another signal."

"Or blow up," I said. "Seems about fifty-fifty, the way our luck runs."

I took a deep breath. All the tests had been fine.

Time to go live.

"Igniting the first bank of engines." I flipped the switch and they rumbled to life. "Second bank igniting."

The ship shook, the vibrations of the engines alone enough to tear the landing struts loose from the years of packed earth.

At least, I hoped so.

"Seal is holding, atmosphere locked in," Hakon reported.

I stared through the canopy at the row of trees before us.

Not exactly ideal if we didn't make it.

"Thrusters set to low," I said, and slowly cranked them up.

A rumble, the shaking grew worse.

Then we were free, the ship hovering above the ground, in flight for the first time in a decade.

Hakon looked over. "Still holding fine. Take her up, Captain."

Carefully I increased the thrust on the engines arranged along the undercarriage of the ship until we were over the tree line, over the mountains.

And still we rose.

"How's the hull holding in section twelve?" I asked Hakon, my eyes busy with my own readouts.

"Holding," he said. "Wouldn't want to go on a months-long voyage in this thing without a better round of refits, but we should be fine for a short system jaunt."

The sky around us changed from pale blue to violet, then to the deepest black as we continued up, breaking through the stratosphere, to the exosphere and beyond into true space.

"We made it," I said, heart throbbing in my chest. "Try the comms again, we shouldn't be getting any interference now."

Hakon opened the comms unit and once again we sent the same message out. "Emergency assistance requested. We have crashed on Sat 9 and require immediate assistance. Please respond if you receive this message."

Immediately, the comms flared to life.

"It's about time." The thin voice of an older man filled the cockpit. "I told them you were far too stubborn to die."

"Thalcorr?" Hakon responded, the stunned tone of his voice enough for me to glance over at him. His eyes were wide as he stared at the unit in front of him.

"You didn't think I was going to return to the Empire having lost you? I've heard about the rest of your family. Rogues and renegades, all."

Hakon's face broke into a wide grin. "I'll be happy to introduce you. But for now, come and get us."

HAKON

As the tractor beam guided us into the docking bay of the *Kodo Ragir*, I looked over at Yasmin.

I'd expected her to relax now that we'd been rescued, now that our survival wasn't hanging on the stability of a ship that had been grounded for years.

But instead, she looked even more tense, chewing the corner of her lip, rubbing the leg pocket of her coveralls over and over.

"You'll like the *Kodo*," I said. "Fantastic food. Beds are far more comfortable than what we found on this thing." I tapped the arm of the co-pilot's seat. "Although I can't argue with the company."

"When will they take us back to Station 112?" she said, eyes fixed straight ahead. "I've got to get in touch with my uncle."

"Easy enough," I said slowly, searching her face for any expression. It was as if everything that happened on Sat 9 had been erased.

This was the Yasmin I'd met before, focused only on her mission.

"As soon as we get on board, I'll have the captain patch you over to your uncle's ship. You can check in, let them know you're okay," I forced a smile. "I'm sure he's been worried."

She glanced over at me, then stared straight ahead again. "Probably."

Right, then. Back to business.

I didn't wait for the thunk of the ship coming to rest inside the docking bay before I moved to the hatch.

When we'd finally settled into place, I went ahead and threw open the door.

Yasmin would come out or not on her own schedule.

Doing it her own way. Just like always.

To my surprise, Ambassador Thalcorr was waiting for us, standing next to Captain Lisi. The captain's eyes raked over the scavenged ship. "Gotta say, doesn't look familiar."

"It's not," I answered her. "But you use the tools you've got. The ship that got us off Station 112 wasn't in any shape to get us back."

"Of course it wasn't," Thalcorr said archly. "Why

would you attempt to ensure that your spacecraft landed in one piece?"

Then his sour face transformed, beaming. "Goodness, my dear," he rushed forward to the hatch, hand extended to help Yasmin down. "Please let me assist you."

It was three steps, for the Void's sake.

But still, I had to fight down a bit of a growl as he solicitously guided her down.

"I'm so sorry my associate didn't let us know that he was accompanied by a guest," Thalcorr continued. "You must be exhausted after your ordeal. We'll have guest quarters set up right away so that you can refresh yourself."

"I need to contact my uncle," Yasmin said quietly, one hand still wrapped around that bag of components and moss, as if it were a talisman. "I want to let him know where I am."

"Of course, of course," Thalcorr said, patting her free hand. "If you crashed on that moon, I'm sure he must be frantic with worry." He bent over her, smile beaming warmth at her. "Where could we reach him?"

The corner of Yasmin's lip quirked up, just a bit. Nice to know she was still in there. "He's probably on Station 112 at this point. It was his flagship attacking it."

"Well..." For a moment, I had the extreme pleasure

of seeing the professional diplomat struggling to maintain his equanimity. "That should make it easy to find him."

"Captain Lisi, can you have one of your people open comms to the station? I'm still certain our guest would like to freshen up while the technicalities are dealt with."

At the slightest movement of Lisi's hand, a freshly scrubbed ensign showed up at her side.

"Escort Miss…"

"Denau," Yasmin supplied.

"Miss Denau to guest quarters, see that she has everything she needs, then at her convenience, bring her to the bridge," Lisi commanded.

After a sharp salute to his captain, the young man bowed to Yasmin.

"If you'll follow me, ma'am."

And she did, without a single glance back.

"I've got things to do," Lisi said. "Including trying to raise that station. Again." And flanked by her juniors, she headed off.

Thalcorr stayed next to me. Waiting.

"You don't seem that worried about me going to freshen up," I said.

He cocked one eyebrow. "From your expression, I assumed you'd do as you please and be just as likely to snarl at me if I suggested such a thing."

Just to piss him off, I didn't snarl.

Even if I felt like it.

While a shower would have been nice, I didn't want to miss any of the action.

Because I had a terrible feeling I knew what was about to happen.

"I can grab something to eat up on the bridge," I decided. "And you can fill me in on what's happened while I was gone."

Thalcorr shook his head as we crossed the docking bay to the lift, stiff posture cracking just a bit. "As I said when I last saw you, Captain Lisi had other plans to remove me safely from Station 112. By the time I was certain there was no peaceful solution possible, she'd sent a small shuttle to retrieve us." He shot a pointed glare in my direction. "I wasn't pleased to report that I had no idea where you were. Serrup was frantic to leave with me, but Alcyon convinced him his place was with his station." A shadow passed over his eyes. "At the time, I agreed."

We stepped out of the lift and onto the bridge.

"Try it again," Lisi told her comms officer, then seeing us, shook her head. "They're still refusing our hails."

"The attacking ships, or the station?" I asked.

"Both. Other than a single transmission, they've gone totally dark."

I punched up a bowl of noodles from the replicator, leaned back, ignoring Thalcorr's grimaces at my slurps, and thought.

"Has Desyk sent any of their own ships to try to relieve the station?"

Thalcorr shook his head. "Not to our knowledge. And I've been unable to reach our original contact at their corporate headquarters."

I finished my noodles, tossed the bowl back in the recycler to be broken down. "There're too many things going on here. And no one is telling us what's happening."

Thalcorr was about to say more, but the door slid back and Yasmin entered the room.

Even knowing she must have rushed, she looked amazing. A tunic of the same shade of blue she'd worn when we met in the hub, but less flowy. Fitted dark pants that drew the eye to her curves, tucked into practical boots. She'd changed the tattered bag made from her coveralls for a slim satchel, probably with the fragments of the uniforms still inside.

I stepped towards her, but she didn't look my way, moving straight to Captain Lisi. "Have you contacted my uncle yet?"

Lisi gestured towards the comms station. "Both the station and the ships are ignoring us, I'm afraid."

Yasmin rubbed her hip, and I assumed that's where

the damn datachip that had started this whole thing was. "Try frequency 364b, please," she said.

At the captain's nod, the communication officer tried again.

Yasmin's lips pressed tight as we waited, a strained white line.

Every instinct I had demanded that I go to her.

But this was something I couldn't protect her from. She wouldn't let me.

"Still nothing, I'm afraid," the officer reported back. "I can keep trying, if you'd like."

Lisi waited expectantly, but Yasmin stepped back and shook her head. "Thank you for your courtesy," she said, nodding to Thalcorr and Lisi. "But if we're not able to establish contact, I must leave and rejoin my uncle."

Thalcorr coughed slightly. "Miss Denau, I really must advise against that."

Yasmin's expression turned to ice. "Are you saying that you won't permit me to leave? An excessive sort of hospitality, I'd say."

"Not at all!" Thalcorr's hands fluttered.

"Just that things on Station 112 seem to be terribly unsettled right now and you possibly don't have all the information. We don't have much more than you do, however." He swallowed tightly and glanced at me. "There's a broadcast you should see, though, before you decide what your next action should be."

Yasmin nodded slowly, eyes still narrowed with suspicion. "That sounds reasonable."

"Captain, may we use your ready room?" Thalcorr asked, then waited for Yasmin to join him.

I followed closely. Whatever this video was that had Thalcorr so unbalanced, it was information. And Yasmin wasn't the only one that needed to know it.

Lisi joined us in the small room that opened off the bridge, and called up a screen that covered one wall.

Before letting the vid play, she paused. "Him, I'm not worried about," Lisi said, pointing to me. "I've never worked with one of his family before, but the fleet knows enough to know they're not delicate flowers. But, miss? This isn't very nice to watch. Are you certain you won't just trust us?"

Yasmin straightened in her chair, her chin held high. "I haven't been a delicate flower for a very long time." Her face softened with a smile. "But thank you. I appreciate the concern."

Thalcorr sat, back to the screen. "I've seen it once. That was enough."

I moved to stand behind Yasmin's chair. She didn't glance at me, didn't acknowledge me.

But I stood there anyway, just in case.

The vid started, the field of view panning around

enough to identify the hub back on Station 112. But instead of the noisy, cheerful chatter that had surrounded us during our dinner, the room was silent.

The tables and booths had been shoved out of the way, and the greenery was torn down.

The largest room on the station was cleared out, and as the camera continued to pan, it was easy to see why.

Rows of gray coverall covered workers clustered together at one end of the room, surrounded by pacing black uniformed guards toting blast rifles.

And on a makeshift stage facing the terrified crowd, stood the old man I'd last seen threatening to blow the observation dome.

Yasmin's uncle.

Ran Denau.

Next to him knelt Commander Serrup. If he'd been racing around in terror during the attack, now he'd shut down completely, eyes wide, staring straight ahead, as if utterly unable to process what was happening.

"Do you care nothing for the people who have been entrusted to you?" Ran Denau asked silkily. He beckoned and one of the guards reached into the crowd and pulled out a man in his thirties.

Nothing remarkable about him other than the look of sheer terror on his face.

"I'm here for information," Denau continued. "But

since you seem to not believe the seriousness of my requests, let me be clear."

With a short hop, he left the stage and strolled over to the unfortunate worker, who had fallen to his knees, mutely shaking his head.

Pivoting quickly, Denau turned back to Commander Serrup.

The camera hadn't zoomed in on the poor fool's face, but it didn't need to for me to read the blankness in his eyes.

"All you have to do is give me the files I want," Denau continued smoothly.

Then without warning, without ultimatums, without counting down, he pulled out a small handheld blaster.

And fired it through the kneeling worker's skull.

Screams from the crowd behind him were quickly cut short at the guards' insistence.

Denau ignored it all.

He moved back towards the stage then stopped, turning again to the crowd.

"Do any of you know where the files are?"

"You bastard!" a blonde woman shoved her way to the front.

She tickled a memory. Maybe she'd been at the table that I'd found Yasmin sitting at in the hub.

My hands clenched uselessly. Whoever she had been, I was certain it wouldn't matter now.

I searched the guards around the crowd, every visible figure of the mercs on the platform for Jenke.

Finally, I spotted him, his face expressionless.

Waiting for something.

"He didn't do anything!" the woman screamed, pulling my attention back. "He didn't know anything. None of us do. We're a fab lab, same as a dozen other places."

"I think not," Denau answered and shot her neatly through the forehead.

There was no screaming that time.

His steps echoing through the hub were the only sounds as he strolled back to the stage and yanked Commander Serrup to the side.

"I really would like those files." Then he stared straight into the camera. "And I will get them."

The screen blanked and we all sat in silence.

Yasmin shook in the chair before me, and I put one hand on her shoulder, rubbing lightly.

And this time, instead of turning away, she reached up and gripped my fingers as if they were the only thing keeping her tethered to reality.

"That's not my uncle," she said softly.

"Yas, honey," I said, still rubbing at her rigid shoulder. "That's the guy that we saw on the ship."

"I know that," she said sharply. "It's certainly his face and his voice. But my uncle is a kind man. He raised us. He would never do something like that. It's Dysek propaganda."

She swallowed and her grip on my fingers grew tighter. "And if it's not, well, I think I have the files he's looking for."

"Even if so, you surely can't mean to give them to him?" Thalcorr protested.

She looked straight at him as the ice grew back over her expression.

But still, she kept her grip on my hand.

"Thank you for your concern. But I really must be leaving now."

"Give the docking bay crew a bit more time to get a ship fueled up and ready, and I'll take you over myself," I said.

Yasmin turned to me, shocked. "Why would you do that?" she said.

"Never finished my tour, did I?"

Besides, we had an ace in the hole.

And he was waiting for us.

I hoped.

L uca waited for us as we exited the Imperial shuttle in the resupply bay of Station 112.

We might be twins, but my brother had always been taller than me, had always been pleased to be just a minute older, enough to claim all the privileges of being the elder.

I hugged him tightly, almost afraid to say anything.

Just happy to be back with my family.

But on the way over from the *Kodo Ragir*, scenes from that disgusting video played over and over in my mind.

Who would've done that? Uncle Ran wasn't like that at all.

And while Grilla certainly had been an obnoxious

individual, she certainly didn't deserve to be killed like that. If she had been killed.

It was propaganda. I'd get to the hub and everyone would be fine.

Just Desyk pushing back against the hostile takeover of one of their stations.

Luca's arms around me stiffened.

"I didn't realize you were bringing guests," he said, his voice the light, politely distant tone he always used around strangers.

I let go and stepped to the side.

"Luca, it's my pleasure to introduce you to Imperial Ambassador Rix Thalcorr."

Thalcorr bowed, no doubt to whatever precise decree protocol demanded.

Unfortunately, it didn't mean much here in the Areitis Sector.

"And this is Hakon," I said, hoping the heat I felt in my cheeks didn't show. "He saved me when my ship crashed after the observation dome was…"

Luca's hand tightened around mine. "I didn't know you were there," he said softly. "I didn't know you were anywhere near Station 112. Neither did uncle. You've got to believe me."

Hakon's eyes narrowed, but he said nothing.

He didn't need to.

I trusted my brother.

"Of course I believe you. It worked out fine." I grinned up at him, unable to suppress the good news any longer. "And I've come back with a present."

His eyebrows rose. "You found the files?"

Nodding excitedly, I tugged his hand, ready to go find Uncle Ran.

In the lift, Luca looked down at me, his expression stern.

"Yasmin, you do know that everything our uncle does is for the good of the corporation, right?"

"Of course," I said, vaguely annoyed at the simple question. "It's our family's legacy. Our honor. We would all do anything for it."

His eyes drilled into mine and for a moment, I felt like there was something he was trying to tell me, some secret message I couldn't decipher.

With a gentle cough, Thalcorr broke in. "I must say, we weren't expecting for there to be quite so much drama on our little visit." He tilted his head gracefully, as he seemed to manage everything. "If your uncle has time, I look forward to speaking to him about the intricacies of this sector. There is so much we have to learn here."

Luca didn't return the smile.

"I don't know what you think you can offer us. I'm

not certain how our uncle feels about your presence, but we've gotten along fine without the Empire for generations."

"Of course," Thalcorr said, ignoring the insult. "But in my career, I found everyone could use more alliances. Terribly useful things, you know."

And Hakon said nothing.

He watched me, watched Luca.

Part of me wanted to stay by his side, safe in his arms, never give up the magic that had sprung between us down on Sat 9.

But here, things were different.

This was the real world.

Luca and Uncle Ran were my real family.

And Hakon?

I'd learn to live without him.

I'd have to.

When the lift door opened, I dashed out, needing some space from the pressure of Hakon's even gaze.

And there was Uncle Ran in the middle of the Command Center, waiting. All the weight and worry of the last few hours flew away as I went straight towards his open arms, ignoring the 'negotiation specialists' stationed around the room, their heavily armed presence startling.

"When they told me you were on board, that you'd

actually been in that observation dome—" his voice broke off and I hugged him tighter.

"It's alright now," I said. "I just don't know why you never got the message that I was here?"

Ran surveyed the technicians deployed along the consoles. "I don't know why, either. But I will." He smiled slightly. "Have no fear of that."

He turned to Thalcorr and Hakon. "I understand I have you to thank for my niece's safety."

Thalcorr stepped forward. "An honor and privilege, Chancellor Denau."

Uncle turned back to me and cupped my chin with his hand. "And I hear you have a present for me? Clever girl."

Unfastening the pocket set into the seam of my pants, I fumbled until my fingers wrapped around the datachip. "I haven't had a chance to examine the files, I'm afraid."

"Well, let's see what they are." He pinched the chip from my grasp and held it out to the side.

Instantly, one of the technicians appeared, took the chip, and scurried away. The technician reported back quickly. "Sir, the files are encrypted."

Uncle's hand moved from my chin and rested lightly around my throat.

"Encrypted? Can you break it?"

"Of course," the hasty reply came. "It just may take us some time."

Hakon growled softly, but loud enough to be heard across the room, as Uncle Ran's fingers tightened.

Then he jerked away.

Dizzy with shock, my hands flew to my throat, the ghostly feel of his fingers lingering.

"Well, niece, perhaps your surprise isn't what we've been looking for after all."

"But I'm sure it is," I said, panicked and confused. "Those were the files buried the deepest in their system, covered with the most security and false trails. Whatever the secret of Station 112, it's got to be in there!"

Instantly, Luca was at my side.

"Uncle, you know that Yasmin is loyal. Everything she has done is for the company."

The anger that had twisted my uncle's face into an unrecognizable mask smoothed away at my brother's words.

"Of course," he said. "You've always been good children, both of you. Loyal. Reliable."

He took a step towards me, and despite myself, I stepped back, the thin worm of doubt that had whittled at my mind in the shuttle forcing itself to the front.

That video hadn't been faked.

And I had no idea what was going on.

I glanced around the room, to find Hakon corralled by one of Uncle Ran's mercenaries.

The two stood face-to-face, equal in height and build, surprisingly evenly matched.

Except for the heavyweight blaster the mercenary carried.

"I'm alright," I called to Hakon, years of practice at hiding any emotion cultivated in endless meetings becoming not just a business tactic, but a shocking matter of survival.

Blaster or no blaster, if he thought I'd been hurt...

My mind stumbled, just a bit.

Hurt by my uncle? That was ridiculous.

I straightened my back and shoved my fears to the back of my mind.

Or at least, tried to.

While Luca stood gravely at my side, Uncle Ran was all smiles now. "The thing is, you'd been gone for so long, no messages, no contact, no progress to report, I was starting to think you had defected."

The bottom fell out of my stomach again. "Of course I haven't," I gasped. "I would never—"

With a wave, he cut me off. "While the data is being decrypted, there's an easy way for you to show me that your loyalty hasn't been swayed." He looked over to where Hakon stood rigid, fists clenched. "By anyone."

I swallowed, throat tight, tongue feeling like

somehow it had swollen to three times its size, choking my words.

"Of course. Anything." I forced my lips into some semblance of the smile I'd worn when the lift first opened.

Had it really been only minutes ago?

Could it really only take minutes to shatter my world again?

"You know I would do anything for you, for the family."

"Then that will make this easy," he answered.

From the pocket of his tunic, he pulled a small blaster.

I stared at it, transfixed, as if it were a venomous thing, strange to see in his hand.

"Well?" he bounced his hand slightly, pushing it towards me. "Take it!" he commanded.

My hands stayed still at my sides, paralyzed by his words.

"And do what?" I whispered.

"Kill one of them." His finger waggled between Thalcorr and Hakon. "I don't really care which."

Thalcorr straightened up in shock. "I beg your pardon?" he snapped. "We are here as part of an official Imperial diplomatic envoy. An attack on us would be—"

One of the mercenaries struck Thalcorr across the

face hard, and Hakon grabbed the ambassador before he hit the floor.

The big mercenary that had blocked Hakon's path to me stepped aside, but he kept his blaster pointed at the two of them.

"The mouthy one or the silent one," the man who had taken me in when my family was destroyed, who I thought of as a second father, shrugged. "Your choice."

My head shook slowly, my mind somehow distant, remote from this horror.

"No."

The sound was no more than a breath.

I repeated it, louder. "No. I'm not shooting anybody."

"Well then, I think my question is answered."

Before I could register the meaning of his words, Ran turned and fired the blaster in one smooth movement.

Hakon leaped in front of the stream, shielding Thalcorr.

"No!" I screamed, struggling to cross the room, but Ran's guards held my arms tightly.

"Put her in quarters where I can get to her later, once we see what she's brought to us."

"What do you want done with those two," the guard nodded towards the corner where Thalcorr was desperately trying to staunch the blood that welled from Hakon's chest.

I couldn't blink, couldn't look away.

Just watch as the life left him.

"Put them in the brig for now. If the big one is meat, shove it through an airlock." Ran smiled with all the warmth of a shark. "They might be useful later. I do like to keep my options open."

HAKON

"Stay still, you idiot."

The words rolled through my brain, meaning-less, echoing.

"I don't even know why you're not dead yet."

I knew that voice. But it wasn't the voice I wanted to hear.

Slowly, I fought my way back to consciousness.

There was something important I had to do, even if I couldn't remember it right now.

"Stay down. Dammit, you've started bleeding again."

I opened my eyes, to find Thalcorr bending over me, his face covered in blood.

The pain radiating through my chest cleared up that question.

My blood.

"What's going on?" I grunted.

Or at least, I tried to, but apparently enough of my meaning got through.

"Quick summary, you've been shot, we've been imprisoned, and your girlfriend has been dragged off somewhere."

My girlfriend.

I struggled to sit up, but Thalcorr easily pushed me back down.

That shouldn't be possible.

"Where is Yasmin?" I demanded.

"I don't know," he snapped. "And I am running out of supplies for bandages to continue trying to keep you alive. I would appreciate it if you'd stay still before I'm completely naked."

"I'd like to avoid that," I said quickly.

For the first time since we'd met, Thalcorr smiled at me.

An actual real smile.

I glanced down, saw a professionally neat bandage wrapping my chest and shoulder.

The only surprise was that it was made out of strips of Thalcorr's diplomatic robes.

"When did you learn to do that?" I asked. "Doesn't seem like something they'd teach along with how to pour the tea."

Thalcorr snorted. "I wasn't born into the diplomatic

corps," he explained as he folded another pad and pressed it lightly over the blaster wound. "I spent half my life as a medic until I realized it would be easier to heal people if I could stop all of those stupid skirmishes from breaking out in the first place."

"Even your voice is different. Where are you from originally?" The words were more difficult now, my brain feeling like it was wrapped up too, muffled.

"Sekjun 5," he admitted. "Not quite the Fringe, but close enough. But the only way to get ahead in the diplomatic corps is to out-snoot the snoots."

"Huh," I muttered. "Glad I didn't throw you out the airlock after all."

"So am I," he answered.

I tried to shift, but the lancing pain put a quick end to that. "Since you've been awake longer than I have, what do you think is going on here?"

"Assuming that the lovely Yasmin didn't lead us into a deliberate trap, I would say that she's terribly misunderstood the nature of her family's corporation." He pursed his lips, thinking. "Or perhaps, just the nature of her family."

"She wouldn't do that," I said.

Doubt wove itself through my thoughts.

Would she?

She'd been willing to do a lot of things for the good of her corp. For the good of her family.

But I'd seen her eyes when I was shot, heard her scream.

No. She hadn't known that would happen.

And there was something else, something important that I needed to remember.

"However, you should sleep now," Thalcorr said, his reassuring hand patting my good shoulder. "You're not going to be able to do anything to help her if you're still bleeding all over the floor." He checked the folded pad, eyes narrowed. "Considering you're not dead, I have to assume that your healing powers are quite amplified."

"Yeah, you could say that." I started to explain Doc's tweaks, but the darkness reclaimed me before I made it through the first sentence.

A SLIGHT SHAKE to my shoulder pulled me back up from the depths.

"I'm terribly sorry," Thalcorr's professional voice was firmly back in place. "I'm certain that a longer period of rest would do you good, but I believe we're about to have company."

I pushed myself to sit upright, the lash of pain that tore through my chest a reminder to not do that again so quickly for a while.

But the old man was right. I took a glance at the

room I'd been unable to focus on before.

Starkly empty. Apparently Station 112 hadn't been designed with a formal brig.

Maybe they'd never had the need.

So Denau had repurposed an old storage room.

Everything that might've been useful had been taken out.

And anything more, I'd have to examine later, because the door was sliding open.

And the first person through was Jenke, his blaster trained on me, his eyes unblinking.

I carefully kept the grin from my face.

Sure, he hadn't been able to break cover before. But now, now we'd get some help.

Behind him came another guard, big, but not as big as we were, carrying a covered tray. The second guard put the tray down at the far side of the room while Jenke kept us covered.

"Denau decided to keep us alive after all?" I said.

"If you survive, you might be useful," Jenke said flatly. "The chancellor likes to keep his options open."

"A blaster hole through the chest doesn't keep most people's options open," I said.

"If he really had wanted you dead, it would've been through your skull," the other guard commented.

That was cheerful.

And put an interesting perspective on Yasmin's

favorite uncle.

Jenke waited for the second guard to rejoin him by the door. "Head on out. I'll catch up with you shortly."

"Protocol demands that—"

Jenke shot the guard a look. "Do you really think either of them are in any shape to take me?" He smiled cruelly. "Besides, the big guy and I have some history. I don't want to miss the opportunity to even a few scores."

The second guard laughed, slapped Jenke on the shoulder, and left the room, sealing the door behind him.

I finally let the grin break through.

"About damn time," I said. "When are we getting out of here?"

Jenke shook his head slowly. "You aren't."

"What?"

"I'm not here to help you," he snarled, his nostrils flaring slightly. "I'm here to make sure you know that. You've been abandoned. Just like we were."

Instinctively I checked the corners where the walls met the ceilings for the telltale glimmer of trackers or cameras.

Jenke saw what I was doing and laughed.

"The room isn't bugged," he spat. "I'm not putting on an act for Denau or ExaTek. I've waited years to have the chance to tell one of you the truth."

I thought the blast to the chest hurt.

I'd been wrong.

"What the hell are you talking about?" I snarled back.

Thalcorr stood, and even in the torn remnants of his robe, managed to look snooty.

Now that I knew it was an acquired expression, I was actually impressed.

"Sir, I'm afraid we haven't been introduced. But let me assure you, that if you have a grievance—"

"Don't bother," I interrupted him. I'd managed to get to my feet, and as long as I stayed leaning against the wall, it seemed likely I would stay there. "This doesn't have anything to do with the Empire. Leave it to me."

Thalcorr nodded and stepped back.

"Nobody abandoned you, or your squad." I forced the words out, the fact that I'd even need to say them aloud bitter on my tongue. "Your messages never got to us. And even if they had, we've been fighting for our lives. The *Daedalus* was lost, most of us were captured, Doc was presumed dead. What mission records survived were salvaged only by the slightest chance."

A muscle in Jenke's jaw twitched. "We were supposed to be a Pack. Brothers," he snarled. "Isn't that what that old bat always said? But instead, we were left to die on our own out here."

"That's not how it was," I insisted. "You don't have all the facts."

"My loyalty is strong. But it's not to you, not anymore."

The bitterness pooled in my gut and my muscles tensed as I prepared to fight.

"Are you here to kill us?" I asked. "Get your revenge?"

He snorted. "No. But I'm not going to help you, either. I wanted to make sure you were clear on that, let it eat you away like it did me when I realized I'd been abandoned."

I started to argue again, then realized I was wasting my breath. Breath that could be used for something more important.

"Fine. But whatever your issue is with the Pack, help Yasmin. She's innocent of whatever bad blood there is between us."

"Denau's niece?" Jenke smirked. "She'll need more than help from just a lone wolf if Denau decides she's been disloyal."

The door sealing behind him closed with an emphatic click.

And I was left to try to make sense of whatever the hell had just happened.

One thing was for certain.

My ace in the hole had turned out to be a joker.

YASMIN

I'd always prided myself on the ability to see things clearly.

To accept reality as it was.

But as I stared at the walls of the executive quarters that had become my prison, I had to wonder.

Had I been lying to myself all these years?

A soft tap at the door caught my attention and I froze.

If it was my uncle, which side of him would it be?

Could I ever trust either of them again after this?

Hakon's body, sprawled in a lifeless tangle of limbs on the Command Center's floor, Ambassador Thalcorr desperately trying to stop the bleeding.

It didn't matter what I looked at it, didn't matter if my eyes were open or closed.

That was all I saw.

The soft tapping came again.

Maybe it didn't matter who it was.

It would never be who I wanted to see, not ever again.

And they hadn't even let me say goodbye.

"Enter," I said, my voice as empty as my chest felt.

But it wasn't my uncle.

I flew at the tall figure, but this time instead of excitement to see him, only rage burned through my veins.

"How could you?" I beat at Luca's chest. "How could you let him do that?"

His arms wrapped around me and, finally, the dam broke. Tears I hadn't let myself cry since I'd been taken away from the bloodstained room in which Hakon had been killed and shoved in the guest quarters, burst out in a torrent.

"I know, Yasmin," Luca said, stroking my hair. "I know. It's not fair."

And all of a sudden, I was twenty again and we had just found our father's body.

"I didn't realize he was going to do that," Luca murmured. "Maybe I should have."

I pushed away from his chest and dashed the tears from my face. "What is happening to our family? What happened to him? How could he change so much?"

Luca led me over to one of the plush chairs in the room's seating area, then rooted through the decorative pillows. Finding one that met his approval, he handed it to me to clutch, the same as I had all through childhood.

I hugged the pillow to my stomach, as if it could keep me afloat in this new sea of lies I found myself cast into.

"I'm not sure he's changed," Lucas said. "I've been with him longer than you, working at his side, even before you disappeared."

"I didn't disappear, I sent a message," I answered. "I don't understand why neither of you got it."

"Uncle might have gotten it," he said. "But he keeps his plans very close to the chest. Always has, even before Father died."

"That's not true," I argued. "He's always told us what he's doing, what his strategies and tactics are, his dreams to rebuild ExaTek."

Luca went to the suite's replicator and punched some buttons.

"For a long time, I thought that, too," he said, then waited while the replicator worked. "Until I started having nightmares."

"Nightmares?" I said. "Recently? Why didn't you tell me?"

"It was a couple years ago, but recently enough. You

were getting your life back on track," he said, shrugging, then handing me a steaming cup of tea, milky and sweet, just the way I liked it.

He kept his black, bitter.

"I realized the nightmares were trying to tell me something," he said, taking the chair facing mine. "And I didn't tell you because, well, if I was wrong, I didn't want to turn your life upside down for no reason."

"But you weren't wrong, were you?"

Luca shook his head. "I don't think so. For the last three years, I've been watching Uncle, trying to separate out what we thought we knew from the truth."

"But what were the nightmares?" I insisted, even though I was afraid I knew the answer.

He took a long sip of tea before answering. "It was the day we found Father. I kept reliving it, night after night, until I realized all of the emotion had been removed from the scene. It was like watching it through a camera lens, like an old vid." Luca met my eyes, and the bleakness in his shocked me. Until I realized that, after the events of the last few hours, my own expression was probably a match for his.

"I started looking at the room where father died more closely," he continued.

I drank my tea; the soothing sweetness I had counted on to relax me now pooling in my gut.

"What did you find?"

"Are you sure you want to know? I know today was hard for you." Luca tilted his head to the side. "Who was he?"

The image of Hakon, bleeding on the floor, covered my vision again.

"I think he would have been my future," I admitted. "I love you. I don't know what to think about Uncle Ran anymore. But I was beginning to think that maybe, maybe there might be something more in the universe for me. But not anymore."

Luca reached for my hand, squeezed my fingers tightly. "Are you sure you want to know the rest right now?" he said. "The only thing is, the way Uncle has been acting, I'm not sure if there'll be a later."

I nodded sharply. "Tell me. I can't afford not to know the truth."

"Then I need you to think back to the day we found father's body. What do you remember of the room when we came in?"

I closed my eyes and found that the burning pain that ripped apart my chest every time I let myself remember anything of that night had dulled.

Maybe there was only so much grief I could handle before it all blended and tangled together.

"Father was in his study," I said, closing my eyes to remember more clearly. "All his terminals had been pulled from the net, backups and comms destroyed. He'd blasted through them, and the smell of burned metal and wires filled the air. We never decided if he was angry at what happened with that woman or despairing." My throat threatened to close, but I swallowed, and cleared it.

This wasn't the time to look away.

"It didn't matter what he'd felt, really. The end was the same."

"What about the blaster," Luca prompted. "What do you remember about the blaster he used?"

"It was so strange," I said. "I hadn't even realized we had one in the house. They always scared me."

"Ever since we were tiny and snuck out to watch scary vids on an unlocked tablet," Luca said. "You never really got over it."

"I don't think I'm likely to now," I said.

"But what did the blaster look like?" he insisted.

I hadn't looked at it closely, hadn't wanted to see the small bit of evil that had taken my father from me.

But I'd seen it, of course, lying on the desk next to Father's outstretched hand.

"It was silver and black," I answered, "smaller than I'd ever expected. Curved at the edges instead of blocky. It might almost have been pretty if it hadn't been so horrible."

"That's right," he said. "That's exactly what it looked like. Now, think about where else you've seen a blaster like that."

"Where else?" I asked, my mind scrambling to comply, but then a sharp rapping sounded at the door.

Lucas rose smoothly, put his teacup back in the recycler, and crossed back over to me.

"Just think about it." One of his rare smiles crossed his face. "And I promise I'll do my best to get you out of here."

He opened the door to reveal the mercenary Hakon had faced off with, before...

Luca nodded his head politely. "Jenke. If you'll excuse me," he said, and slipped out into the corridor.

The mercenary watched him leave with narrowed eyes, then came into the room.

Tossing aside the pillow, I ran to him. "You know," I faltered, and restarted, "knew Hakon, didn't you?" I said, then I took a good look at his face, the sharp features, the slightly pointed ears.

And the truth struck me.

"You didn't just know Hakon," I said softly. "You're one of his brothers, aren't you?"

His eyebrows raised slightly. "We were grown in neighboring tanks, if that's what you're talking about. But it doesn't mean anything."

"But that can't be true," I said, thinking about myself and Luca. "Ran killed your brother. How can you keep working for him?"

Jenke's lips twisted. "He shot somebody I used to know, that's all." He turned away to wander through the room, his sharp eyes covering everything.

"What are you doing? What are you looking for?"

"Making sure you don't have a way to escape," he said. "I've been put in charge of your confinement until your uncle decides what to do with you."

"Then you can get me out of here," I gasped. "Or at least get Ambassador Thalcorr back to his ship. He doesn't have anything to do with this. We don't even know why Desyk reached out to the Empire, sent them here to this station. It's nothing to do with ExaTek or Uncle Ran."

Jenke snorted. "I'm not getting anybody out of anything." He sighed, leaning against the wall. "Look, you seem like a nice enough lady. But here's the truth. I'm paid to do a job." He pointed at me. "I'm paid to make sure you stay put. So you're gonna stay put."

"But what happened to Hakon. He was your brother," I pressed. "Doesn't that mean anything to you?"

"Not anymore." Some emotion I couldn't place flashed across his eyes, then was gone, so quickly I might've imagined it.

"Life is full of pain and betrayal," Jenke said. "I would've thought you would have learned that by now. But if you haven't, learn it quickly. It's all that will save you in the end."

HAKON

"What's the plan?" Thalcorr asked, warily eyeing the door, obviously preparing himself for whatever the next unpleasant surprise was going to be.

"It's not really much of a plan," I admitted. "We wait until I heal up a little more, bust out of here, trash everything we come across until we find Yasmin, and get out."

"You're not going to do anything about your... friend who was so kind to come visiting?"

I shot him a dirty look. "I can't make him listen to the truth. If he thinks he was abandoned." I shrugged, glad that this time didn't hurt as much as the last. "His team was sent to the Areitis Sector on a mission. I don't have the details. I was in the field myself when they went. But then everything went pear-shaped on our end. They weren't abandoned, but it probably feels like that to them."

It wasn't that I didn't sympathize with Jenke.

Even at the worst of it, when we'd been captured and tortured by the Hunters, when we'd known our home was gone and Doc had been killed, when I was damn sure there was no way out, I'd known my brothers had my back.

There weren't a whole lot of things in the universe that I believed in, but I'd never had to question that faith.

And in the end, that faith had been validated. We'd been rescued. We'd won our battle, back in the Empire.

But that didn't mean anything to Jenke.

"When we get back to Orem, I'll have one of his old teammates get a message to him. Maybe he'll listen to Torik."

Unless Torik felt the same, and was just better at hiding it.

Stupid people with their stupid, complicated emotions.

Give me a machine I could tear apart any day.

"Either way, that's not the mission right now. Getting all of us out of this trap is going to be enough of a challenge for one day."

Yasmin's scream still echoed in my ears. She was

still out there, the man she'd trusted more than anything, a killer.

She was the only mission now.

Examining the ceiling for weaknesses while still leaning heavily on the wall for support, only the slightest whisper from the back of the room gave me an indication that we weren't alone.

"I'm sorry to hear you're planning on leaving so soon," Alcyon said as a panel slid away to reveal a darkened passage. "I'd hoped I could convince you to give us a hand here, in exchange for getting you out in a less dramatic fashion."

His gaze took in the bandages wrapped around my chest, the blood half dried. "You're in better shape than I expected. That's probably for the best." He beckoned for Thalcorr and me to follow him. "But no matter what shape you're in, we should hurry before you get another visitor."

After my first two halting steps, I only half-grumbled when Thalcorr moved under my arm to bear some of my weight.

"You're heavier than you should be," he grunted as we crossed the room to join Alcyon at the hidden door.

"Reinforced skeletal structure," I answered. "If you want to know any more, you'll have to ask Doc. I don't know most of the details about how we were built, just how it lets me survive."

"And a good thing, too," Thalcorr replied.

Three steps into the darkened corridor, automatic lights flickered on knee-high, lighting the way.

"While I'm glad to be out of there," I said, "want to tell me where we're going? And why are you not under guard with Commander Serrup?"

"Let's get going," Alcyon answered as he headed deeper into the passage. "I'll fill you in on the way. It's a bit of a trip, and there are no lifts in here."

It was hard to get a mental map running of where we were going, since I hadn't exactly been conscious when we were dumped in the storage room.

BUT THE INCREASED HUMMING of machinery and the slight changes in gravitational pull gave me a hint. We were heading closer to the central axis of the station.

And with every minute, I could feel the strength returning to my body. Not as fast as it would have if I'd had the sense to lay down and sleep, but that wasn't exactly an option.

"I guess we're about to find out what's taking up space on all those hidden floors," I said.

Maybe it was petty of me to be quite so happy to see Alcyon freeze in his tracks, but it had been a crappy day.

He whirled back towards me. "You did crack that

data," he said accusingly. "I haven't been able to recreate everything, but during the attack, I got the alert those files had been accessed."

"Not by me," I laughed, then stood a little straighter, balancing my weight gingerly as I tested moving my shoulder around. "I never was in your files in the first place."

"Then how did you know?" He didn't sound like it was going to be easy to convince him I'd had nothing to do with those files.

Suspicious people were a pain in the ass.

"Lucky guess, backed up with a good sense of spatial measurements," I answered, not really caring anymore if he believed me, but willing to make the effort in the hope that he'd volunteer some much-needed information in return. "You had way too much space in this thing for the number of people and labs you were running." I waved him on and he reluctantly continued down the sloping walkway.

"A station with too much space, an exploratory ship on a nearby moon that never came back, and rumors of secrets interesting enough that the heir to your rival corporation decided you needed to be infiltrated." Alcyon muttered something, but I didn't catch it. "It didn't even need the attack by Denau on your supposedly lowly little fabrication station to give me a clue that there was something else going on here."

ELIN WYN

Finally, he stopped and entered a long series of digits into a recessed panel, then slid his hand into the slot that opened up.

"And here we thought we'd been clever, requesting the Imperial ambassador meet us here rather than at Dysek headquarters," he said. "We thought it would keep ExaTek out of our business."

Another door slid open and finally we stepped into the real Station 112.

Thalcorr stepped forward, still annoyingly regal in his rags. He took in the vast engineering complex with one sweeping gaze. "I see that the Emperor should've sent a team of engineers with us."

"I'm not exactly a team, but I can probably follow along," I said.

I shook my head at his look of mild surprise. "I'm not just a pretty face, you know. I'm pretty good at this stuff."

Not that I was entirely certain what this stuff was, in this case.

But I'd figure it out.

The back of the room was filled with gigantic canisters, filled with swirling colors. Something about the shifting patterns reminded me of something, but I couldn't put my finger on it.

Alcyon walked to the central console and pulled up a display. "I had a feeling when you ran your little test on our fabrication design team that you had an engineering background," he said. "Tell me what you think about this."

He flipped out a 3D holographic model of... something and sent it across the room to me.

I looked at the schematics, pulled apart everything I could.

Studied it again, and thought about how it could be used.

"You don't need an engineer for this, Thalcorr. You need a physicist. Maybe a chemist. Or both." I pulled open the diagram for one of the canisters, looking for more clues. "I don't know how they're doing it, but I can tell you what they're ending up with. Whatever they're compressing, they're putting it into high-density fuel cells." I tapped one and sent it spinning through the air back toward Alcyon. "And that's all well and good, but it doesn't get me closer to getting Yasmin out of this snake pit."

"You're quite correct," Alcyon nodded. "Using a proprietary formula that we acquired a number of years ago, we've been able to convert the atmosphere of the gas giant below us into high-powered fuel. The process is unique."

That would explain why the swirl of colors looked familiar.

Normally, it would be fascinating. Normally, I'd

want to take the whole thing apart, put it back together, see how it could all be improved.

Now, there were other things on my mind.

"Don't care. Where's Yasmin?"

"You don't want to know more about what she was willing to risk so much to discover?" he answered. "Our company is willing to offer our process to the Empire at a discount in exchange for trading considerations." Alcyon tilted his head slightly. "Of course, given the current set of complications, if the Empire could see its way to assist us, we would be prepared to make the process available at even more of an attractive price."

"No, really," I said. "I don't care. Right now, he doesn't care either. No," I said, interrupting Thalcorr as he was opening his mouth. "You don't." Stretching out my shoulders, I took my first full breath in hours. Good enough. Walking slowly towards Alcyon, I did my best to make our position clear. "You seem to have eyes on every bit of this station, even the hidden bits. Where. Is. Yasmin?"

"And I must ask," Thalcorr insisted. "Where is poor Commander Serrup? Has Chancellor Denau already disposed of him?"

Alcyon shook his head. "No, he is still confined to quarters. Denau won't get anything useful out of him, but probably thinks it's worth it to keep him as a hostage." His lips twisted into a half-smile. "You thought it was a joke that I was in charge of Station 112. But it's been nothing but the truth. Serrup was part of the disguise. He never knew anything about the real work that happened here."

With a complicated wave over the console, the entire system lit up. And I could see it now, the gas from one canister moving to the next, molecules stripped and reconfigured as they went.

"Serrup didn't have the math for it," Alcyon continued. "And even if he did, he didn't have the spine to stay quiet."

"So you abandoned him," I said flatly.

"I put the corporation first," Alcyon said simply. "I always have."

What was it with these people in this damn sector? I wondered.

Yasmin, her uncle, this guy.

They all seemed to be perfectly rational people.

Well, not Yasmin's uncle, he was obviously a homicidal maniac.

But when it came to their damn corporations, they lost all sense of perspective.

Thalcorr stepped forward. "While I am certain that your process is ingenious and invaluable, I don't believe that we can negotiate with you until all our party has been safely removed to our ship."

I shot him a look and he waved it away.

"Of course, by defining all our party, I am including Yasmin Denau. Once she has rejoined us, if she wishes to return here, that would be acceptable. But we will not initiate negotiations without her."

Huh.

Maybe there was something to this whole diplomacy business.

"Fine," Alcyon said. "She's been confined to quarters, much nicer quarters than when she was embedded here as a worker."

He swiped the model away, pulled up a new screen, and started flipping through security feeds. "See, she's right here."

The cameras displayed multiple views of a suite. It must've been set aside for visiting officers from Desyk or other VIPs. It just had one problem.

"It's very nice," I agreed. "But she's not there."

"What?" Alcyon quickly started flipping through camera feeds.

But Yasmin was gone.

YASMIN

Pain and betrayal.
　　I stared at the door long after Jenke had left, my mind racing.

The pain that had racked me when Uncle Ran shot Hakon threatened to overwhelm me again, knees buckling, gut twisted into knots.

Before today, I'd never seen, never imagined Uncle Ran with a blaster in his hand.

That blaster, small and almost elegant.

Even in the vid, he'd been so comfortable with it, accurate. Lethal.

Practiced.

Then realization struck me, and I ran to the privacy closet to be sick.

The blaster. That's what Luca had been saying.

I pulled the images up in my imagination one after the other, the blaster that had been on my father's desk, the blaster in Uncle Ran's hand.

They were the same.

Lots of blasters look like, I told myself as I rinsed my mouth out, staring at myself in the mirror, my eyes dark pits now, smudges underneath making me look exhausted, ancient.

I *felt* ancient.

It couldn't be anything more than a coincidence.

Maybe a present, or an heirloom from my grandparents, maybe both brothers had been given one.

Except…

Why had I never known there was a weapon in the house?

Father had been so careful with our safety, surely he would have gotten rid of such a thing or at least warned us of its presence.

And there was no reason for Uncle Ran to have…

I stopped, and forced myself to think the words.

To have killed Father.

He'd always said he never wanted to be the leader of ExaTek, that he was happy to help his older brother, be the man behind the scenes.

I barely remembered our grandparents, but they'd doted on our father. Everyone seemed to agree that Father was the best person to lead the company.

Luca had to be wrong.

But what else did he know?

He wouldn't have hinted so strongly about Uncle's guilt in our father's death if it was just the similarity of the blasters.

Luca had been at Uncle's side for years. What else had he seen to make him suspicious?

Whatever it was, I wasn't going to find out stuck in here.

Glancing around the room for cameras, I finally decided it didn't matter.

I'd have one chance to do this and I had better be fast.

Bending over as if to adjust my shoe, I opened up the hidden pocket in the deep hem of my pants.

There hadn't been much time to program up replacement clothing with such specific alterations in those few moments I'd been alone on the *Kodo Ragir*.

But it had been long enough, even to redistribute the contents of the makeshift bag. The precious salvaged components that had seemed so important for so long, I'd dumped into the recycler without a second thought.

The fragments of the Dysek uniforms, I'd folded and placed carefully into the newly made satchel with a sample of the moss.

The datachip had gone into a pants pocket.

And the access card I'd kept all this while, wrapped in Hakon's shredded jacket nestled in the bottom of the bag, I'd hidden most carefully of all.

Thankful for the impulse that had urged me to not slide it into the satchel that had been ripped from me before I'd been deposited unceremoniously into this suite, I hid the card in my palm.

Wandering to the replicator, I opened the menus as if I was browsing for something to eat, and crossed my fingers.

I'd never been able to look into the system before, never had the right access except for that brief moment when I'd had the card in my hand with Hakon at the hub.

Where we'd had our first meal together and even despite my focus on the mission, I hadn't been able to stop myself from basking in his warmth.

I pushed that memory away.

I'd take it out again later, when I had the answers I needed. When his friend Thalcorr was safely out of this place.

Hakon and I hadn't had much time together, but there were plenty of memories. They would have to be enough to last me for a lifetime.

Brushing away tears, I worked deeper into the operating code of the replicator, followed the path the system used to monitor and replenish stocks, until I was deep into the systems of Station 112 itself.

The tiny screen wasn't built to display camera feeds, but it would do.

It would have to.

First steps first.

I needed to get out of this room, because if Uncle Ran decided I wasn't loyal, I had no doubts what would happen to me.

The camera showed Jenke outside the door, watching and waiting as if he had all the time in the world. There was no sound, but just having some sense of what was happening outside was a relief.

But I didn't have the time Jenke had. Splitting the tiny screen, I kept one eye on him while flipping through cameras, trying to find Thalcorr.

With luck, I could get him back to his shuttle.

If he couldn't pilot, I'd take him back to the *Kodo Ragir,* then return in the old exploratory shuttle Hakon and I had made it off of Sat 9 in. I'd come back to find Luca, and get solid answers instead of hints.

It wasn't a great plan, but it was something.

But no matter where I looked, I couldn't find Thalcorr.

Suddenly, another mercenary came running into view on the other screen, his quick gestures matching the anxious expression on his face as he said something to Jenke.

With a glance back at my door, Jenke followed the newcomer, leaving the corridor empty, trusting in the lock to keep me in.

"Mistake number one," I muttered as I slipped out, hurrying in the opposite direction to the one they'd taken.

The executive suites were only a few levels away from the fabrication labs, and I made my way slowly to my old workspace.

There'd be no reason for anyone to look for me there, and the terminals would let me search the station in safety while I made my plans.

It would be the perfect hiding place.

The door slid open, and Tinon's mouth dropped open, mirroring mine.

"What are you doing here?" we both whispered as I scuttled inside, sealing the door behind me with the access card.

"You've been missing for days!" Tinon continued. "Rumor was that you'd been blown off the station in the attack."

"That's sort of what happened," I admitted. "But I'm here now. I just need to be quiet about it, alright?"

Tinon snorted. "I wasn't exactly an eager trandor to get my hours in before we switched corps. With the new management, I want to keep my head down and not get killed."

Swallowing hard, I nodded. For most of the workers here, it was just another hostile takeover.

Maybe with a slightly higher body count, but really, it wasn't unknown for a takeover to have a few rough days in the beginning.

Grilla and Urtu would have had a different take on it, I was sure.

But Uncle Ran's method had certainly managed to motivate Tinon.

"It's all a little complicated," I said. "Right now, I'm just looking for information."

"Don't have any," he said hurriedly. "I'm just making sure I hit my quota. I don't hear or see anything."

The blare of an alarm rang through the room.

All workers! Assemble in the hub in ten minutes for corporation announcements.

Tinon went pale, hands shaking as he powered down his station.

"What's wrong?" I asked. "What sort of announcements could be that bad?"

"I've been keeping my numbers up, but you never know," he muttered.

"Never know what?" Dread pooled in my stomach.

"Who he's going to punish," Tinon whispered, eyes darting from side to side. "Were they behind on their numbers? Were they talking out of turn, too loyal to the old corp? Don't know why, one corp is the same as the other, really."

Punish.

I thought back to the vid of the assembly, where Uncle Ran had so easily killed Grilla and Urtu.

I hadn't liked either of them, but they hadn't deserved to die just for talking back.

And no one had tried to stop him.

Tinon stood, brushing off his coveralls as if anything would make him look more presentable.

"I need you to help me," I decided quickly.

"No, I need to go. I can't be late." He swallowed hard, looking trapped.

But there was no other way.

"Just give me a hand getting the housing off the laser cutter," I insisted.

This had to end.

And it was up to me to do it.

"This isn't a good idea, this isn't a good idea," Tinon muttered over and over, but I ignored him. He was helping me, and that was all that mattered.

We'd taken the housing off the laser cutter assembly often enough for cleaning. Even in his panic, his hands knew the routine and broke down the components without thinking.

Safety housing, secondary casing, and finally the cutter was loose.

"Alright," I said softly. "You can go."

But now that he had been freed, Tinon stayed still, feet rooted to the floor, his eyes fixed on the laser cutter.

"What are you going to do?" he whispered.

"Take care of some family business," I said, pulling the laser cutter free, and placing it on my workbench. "I can make the rest of the adjustments myself," I said. "Go on, you don't want to be late."

He swallowed repeatedly, opened his mouth as if to ask more questions, then decided better of it.

"Good luck," he said as he turned away. "I think."

I couldn't rely on luck. My hand froze as I started to make the final adjustments.

I hated blasters, had never touched one.

But someone had to do something. And apparently, that someone was me.

I got to work.

Half an hour later, I carried the heavy cutter at my side as I ghosted down to the hub.

The video I'd seen on the *Kodo Ragir* played over and over in my mind. But this time, I wasn't focused on what Uncle Ran had been doing, or Grilla's scream of terror and outrage echoing in my ears.

This time, I was trying to remember what the rest of the room had looked like.

The booths and tables, the greenery-draped arches that had been set up to give some semblance of privacy, had all been knocked down and pushed to the sides.

In one corner, it looked like the debris had been piled high enough that it should give me cover.

At least, if nothing had changed.

The months on the station where I'd kept to myself, watched and waited, exploring on my own without being seen, were paying off now.

I could hear Uncle Ran ranting before I even got to the hub, slipping toward the corridor doors which would come out as close as possible to my target corner, his words blaring from the loudspeakers.

"There can be no dissension! Loyalty to ExaTek is all!"

I stopped, fighting to slow my heart rate and calm my breathing before I took the last few steps out of the corridor and into the open space of the hub.

I crouched down and dashed across the floor, but I didn't need to worry.

All eyes were on Uncle Ran.

Slowly, carefully, I maneuvered the laser cutter until the tip protruded slightly from the barricade of discarded furniture.

"And yet, despite my trust in you, you have failed me," Uncle Ran boomed out from the stage.

He strode back-and-forth, his face red and twisted. I gnawed at my lip, willing him to stand still so I could get a clear shot. At least Luca wasn't up there with him.

I wouldn't be able to do this more than once. Even if his guards didn't find me and stop me before I could try again, I wasn't sure I'd have the strength to pull the trigger twice.

Finally, Uncle Ran spun on his heel, arm outstretched, his finger pointing accusingly at the man standing before him.

"Not only did you fail ExaTek, you failed me! You were one of my most trusted men. I believed in you." His voice dropped to a menacing whisper. "And yet you let her go."

The guards raised their blasters, so many against one lone man.

My hand fell away from the trigger.

Jenke. He was going to execute Jenke because I'd managed to escape.

Jenke with all of his hurt and bitterness.

Hakon's brother.

Even if I shot Uncle Ran now, the rest of his guards could kill Jenke in seconds.

"No!" I shouted as I scrambled out from behind the overturned furniture. "I'm right here. Let him go."

Jenke whirled around, eyes wild. "What in the Void are you doing?" he snarled as Uncle Ran signaled, and a group of guards rushed towards me.

But for all I cared, Jenke and I were alone in the room.

"You were wrong," I said. "Yes, there's plenty of pain and betrayal in the universe."

For a moment, I could see Hakon's handsome features superimposed on Jenke's, but then they blurred and went away.

"But there's love, too. You're his brother," I tried to explain as the rest of the guards moved to circle me as well. "I couldn't save him. But I can save you."

HAKON

"What do you think you're doing?" I growled at Thalcorr, my eyes fixed on Yasmin, just as they had been ever since she emerged from behind the turned over tables across the hub.

"Do you think you can save her, get her out of this, all by yourself?" he asked sadly.

"It doesn't matter," I said. "I have to at least try."

Alcyon smirked. "If you're going to bother to charge in there, it would make sense to me to make sure you get her out alive. What do I know? I've never been much of one for romance." He pulled out a comm unit and started tapping. "There's over forty guards out there. Denau has kept them with him at all times since he took the station. You can't count on the workers helping, but if you give me a minute, I could increase the odds a bit."

Pushed and prodded by the guards, Yasmin strode through the crowd to stand next to Jenke, who stepped between her and her uncle.

"She's your blood," he spat out. "Your kin. I was derelict in my duties, she escaped." He tilted his head to the side slightly. "More points to her for cleverness, I'd say."

Yasmin put one small hand on his shoulder. "It won't work," she said. She moved to stand by his side. "Uncle, your guard was loyal. I was here long enough to learn the Desyk systems. I let myself out. No one has betrayed you."

Denau's face twisted in rage. "If you were loyal, you wouldn't have run," he said. "The data on the chip was valid. You would've been at my side, a heroine to the cause. But instead, you chose to leave the room where I'd placed you for your own safety. Why?"

Before she could answer, one of the guards approached the stage. "Sir, we found this back where she was hiding." The man held a long, bulky, clumsy cylinder, slightly tapered.

It took me longer than it should have to realize what it was.

Denau had no trouble. "A laser cutter," he laughed. "Darling niece, did you really think you could kill me?"

"That's it. Time to go," I whispered to Alcyon. "Whatever you're going to do, now's the time."

"My men will be in position in two more minutes," he argued. "You can wait until then."

I shook my head. "I wouldn't trust that mad bastard to refrain from killing everyone in the room for that long." Stretching out my shoulder one last time, I decided the chest wound was healed enough.

It would have to be.

"Hey, Denau!" I shouted as I sprang over the barricade. "You've got more holes in your security than you tried to put in me."

Jenke's mouth twisted into a half smile, and I nodded in acknowledgment.

Denau sputtered. "How are you here?"

I moved closer to the stage, closer to Yasmin, even as the crowd of unarmed workers shrank back.

Two of Denau's guards rushed me. Suckers.

In moments, they were out cold on the floor, and their blasters had been tossed back to Alcyon and Thalcorr.

"Apparently, after you pulled in this guy for not keeping a close enough eye on your niece, no one felt like telling you I'd gone for a stroll myself." I risked a quick glance at Yasmin, forced myself to keep the easy, relaxed pace instead of rushing to her side. Her eyes shone, and her hands were clamped over her mouth.

"Sorry for the surprise, mate. Your uncle wasn't the only one trying to find you."

"We'll talk about appropriate surprises later," she managed to croak out, and the smile on her face made every lingering pain worth it.

"I hear flowers are traditional," I offered, keeping an eye on Denau. He looked like he'd short-circuited, head pivoting between us. Maybe it had been too long since anyone had dared go against his plans.

Maybe he wasn't used to being interrupted mid-rant.

Either way, I was halfway to my mate, where I could touch her, protect her.

"What if I want glowing mushrooms instead?" Yasmin answered, the teasing lightness in her voice not quite covering the tension.

"No." Just a few more yards and I'd be at her side. "I'm drawing the line at mushrooms. Or giant purple dinosaur things. We can discuss moss or flowers, your choice."

And Denau snapped. "Kill them, kill them all!" he screeched. "All three of them, traitors and spies!"

Before the words had finished leaving his mouth, Jenke grabbed the nearest guard, planted a fist in the man's face, and swung the unconscious body in a circle, clearing a space around where he and Yasmin stood, the rest of the guards scrambling back in shock.

"Glad to see you're on our side," I shouted as I leaped into the fray, slamming into guards at high speed, taking out as many as possible on my way to Yasmin.

"Not sure about you yet," Jenke answered, pulling a blaster off one of the guards and tossing it to me. "But I like her."

"Thanks," Yasmin said, as she darted to stay out of the line of fire. "But maybe we could do the family reunion after we're out of here?"

"Hey," I took out two more guards, covering another few yards towards her. "We're not the only ones with a dysfunctional family dynamic here."

"Your mate, huh?" Jenke answered. "Good choice."

"And we're talking about that, too," Yasmin shouted, stripping another blaster from an unconscious guard and handing it to Jenke.

Weaving between the next wave of guards, I rolled low, then sprang up, toppling the next idiot in my path.

A shot over my shoulder caught a guy I hadn't noticed.

"Don't get cocky," Thalcorr shouted from behind the barricade, then took aim at the next one.

I kept the next one's blaster, and continued battling my way through.

For all his talk, Alcyon's numbers were wrong. This

was more than forty, but there was no stopping to count now.

But finally, I was at her side.

"Cover us," I asked Jenke gruffly, and pulled Yasmin to me, needing to touch her, to know she was real, to know she was safe.

At least for now.

"Survive now, make out later," Jenke said. "Congratulations, by the way. I'm pretty sure you don't deserve her."

Yasmin's fingers trailed down my jaw before she pulled away. "We have so many things you're going to be explaining. Don't think I'm not making a list."

Jenke and I took back-to-back positions, circling with Yasmin in the middle, protecting her as well as we could in a room full of hostiles.

"Tell me you've got an endgame for this," Jenke said. "We're wearing them down, but it only takes one lucky shot."

"My guy says his people should be in position any time," I grunted.

"How many people does he have?"

"No idea," I admitted, spinning to kick away another guard that had gotten too close. "Not enough that he was willing to risk them without a little help."

CLANG!

All across the far wall of the hub, panels fell down,

revealing a dozen helmeted guards in dark blue uniforms, the shrieks of the huddled workers adding to the chaos.

"Shit!" Jenke said. "Doesn't it ever let up?"

"I think they're on our side," I answered.

"Think?" Yasmin cut in. "How are we going to know?"

"I guess it depends if they start shooting at us or not," Jenke said. "You might want to add this to the list of things to talk to your mate about when you get him somewhere safe."

It might only have been a dozen, but since Denau's guards had been focused so intently on us, Alcyon's troops had a temporary advantage.

The newcomers pressed forward, and Jenke and I pivoted slightly, trapping Denau's guards between us. Within seconds, they were whittled down to just a few men caught in the crossfire, then the dwindling enemy started to panic.

"I think we're going to pull it off," I called over my shoulder to Yasmin.

But a cut-off scream was the only answer.

I whirled, chest tight, my heart thundering in my ears.

And the worst had happened.

Denau had taken advantage of the confusion to snatch Yasmin from behind our backs, leaning over the edge of the stage to take her from the one direction we hadn't expected.

Above.

Now he held her struggling on the stage, the same small blaster he'd used on me now pressed against her head.

"Lose your weapons!" he commanded.

Instantly, Jenke and I dropped our blasters.

"I can still take him," Jenke muttered, so low that no one else in the room would've heard it.

I only had eyes for Yasmin's terror. "We can't risk it. Wait for the moment."

"I said drop them!" Denau repeated and, likely signaled by Alcyon from behind the barricade, I heard the clatter of Desyk's troops disarming.

"Did you really think you could fight back against me?" Denau sneered. "I am always prepared; I was always the smarter one. No one had faith in me, but I proved them all wrong."

I glanced at Yasmin, hoping she had some idea of what he was raving about.

"You've always been a good leader of ExaTek," she whispered. "I just don't understand why you're doing this."

He shoved the blaster harder against her temple and she flinched.

"Because you've never had to struggle for anything,"

he snarled. "Everything has been given to you, just like it was to Kenth. Unlike my brother, I had to fight for what I wanted."

"Father?" she squirmed in his grasp and I held my breath, willing the blaster not to go off. "What about Father?"

"He was a fool, a coward," Denau said. "And—"

Yasmin kicked back, catching him in the knee and rolling away.

Or at least, she tried to.

Before she could move far enough, Denau fired.

"No!" I roared, charging the stage.

But he'd already grabbed her arm again, dragging her back across the stage as she stumbled, blood streaming down from the wound in her thigh.

"I'm going to kill you," I promised him, forcing myself to stay still, to not endanger Yasmin.

"You might not get the chance." Yasmin's brother rose from the back of the stage, and in two quick strides had another blaster, the twin of the one Denau held, shoved against Denau's neck. "Let her go, Uncle."

With a twist of his lips, Denau nodded, conceding defeat, then pushed Yasmin away. He dropped the blaster, his arms hanging limply at his sides.

"I always saw you had potential, my boy," he purred.

"I'm not your boy," Luca said flatly. "You think we've never fought for things? Yasmin and I fought to have some sense of normalcy after you destroyed our family. I've fought for years to get information, to keep the smile on my face when working with you. I've fought, suspecting, until I finally knew the truth."

Denau's eyebrows raised, but he said nothing as Yasmin darted forward to grab the blaster and shove it away from her uncle's feet.

"Yas, get away!" I hissed, but even from a distance I could see that that small movement had obviously pained her, her pale face screwed up in agony.

"I've got to get some med seal on that," I muttered. "She's not like us, won't heal for days."

"Good thing, too," Jenke answered. "I expect she's saner."

"My boy," Denau put emphasis on the word, dragging it out. "All that time, you thought I never wondered?" Moving like a snake, he ducked down and to the side, reaching up to snatch the blaster from Luca's hand, then pistol-whipping Yasmin's brother twice until he fell into a bloody heap at Denau's feet.

"You're both idiots," Denau said, lip curling. "I should've expected it. Our parents always thought your father was the golden child. 'So handsome, so smart, so perfect.'" The mocking words twisted his face. "But he couldn't do what needed to be done. I could see that, even back then." He kicked Luca, hard. "I'd hoped that I would have had more influence on you, but your father's weaknesses ran through you both." His hand rose, blaster aimed at Yasmin. "No matter, it ends now."

I dove for Yasmin, pulling her into my chest and rolling away, covering her with my body.

The smell of scorched flesh filled the air.

But it wasn't mine.

"I'm here, I'm here," I murmured, pushing the hair back from her face. "It's over now."

"He killed him," she said, still stunned. "He killed our father just to take the company."

"I know, babe. I know."

I glanced over my shoulder.

Denau's body sprawled awkwardly on the stage. Jenke's shot had gone cleanly through Denau's forehead, and Jenke was already checking on Luca.

"Kid'll be fine."

Thalcorr ran across the room, pushing me away from Yasmin, flinging down a med kit he'd found somewhere next to her. "Let me see that leg," he insisted. "You can fawn over each other all you want later."

Whatever. I kept hold of her hand.

While he worked, I scanned the room.

Led by Alcyon, the Desyk troops regained their weapons and corralled the surviving ExaTek guards into a corner of the hub.

Knowing human nature, it wouldn't take long for

the previously terrified workers to be lending a hand, enthusiastically taking the chance to have a little revenge against their tormentors.

"Well, I guess we can get back to the business of negotiations," Alcyon said, leaving his men in control of the crowd. "We like—"

Then the speakers went live, a deep rumbling voice echoing through the room, through the very metal of the station.

Open message to whoever the hell is running that place. If somebody doesn't tell me where my men are right NOW, I'm going to come over there and tear you apart with my bare hands. You have ten seconds to answer.

And I'll help! A second, chipper, voice added.

Jenke looked at me, jaw slack, eyes wide with shock. "Was that…"

"Ronan," I nodded. "Sent a message to him that you were here before we came back over." I rubbed my eyes. "I'll explain Nixie later."

"Another of your brothers?" Yasmin asked blearily as the painkillers kicked in.

"Yeah," I stroked her cheek as her eyes closed and she relaxed into sleep. "You'll meet him in a little bit, I'm sure." I met Jenke's gaze. "I told you, we don't abandon anyone."

EPILOGUE: YASMIN

"Are you sure you're okay?" Luca asked for the fourth time since he'd come into the room.

"You want to take the bandage off and check it?" I asked. "Ambassador Thalcorr did a great job with the field dressing. The woman who came over on that new ship, Nadira? She's a fully qualified doctor. She re-examined it, says I should be up and moving in a couple of days." I narrowed my eyes at him, the swollen side of his face distorting the line of his jaw. "You're not looking so hot yourself."

"I just...I didn't think you'd end up in the middle of everything," he said quietly, his shoulders curved in as if to ward off another blow.

I patted the bed. "Come, tell me about it. Everything."

ELIN WYN

Instead, he went to the replicator and made two cups of tea, waiting until I'd pushed myself more upright before handing one to me.

Dragging a comfortable looking chair closer to the bed, he sat, gazing into the steaming cup, but stayed silent.

As he must have been for years.

"When did you begin to suspect Ran?" Even now it hurt to say our uncle's name. It was too hard. His actions had made the ties of family into a mockery, a travesty.

"Not for years," he said. "But once I started working closely with him, I started seeing a side of him I hadn't imagined."

"You shouldn't have had to handle that by yourself," I said.

"It's what we both wanted," he argued. "I was going to learn the ropes, and you were going to put that engineering degree to use inspecting and improving our manufacturing facilities. That was the plan even before..."

Before everything had fallen apart.

"But it wasn't Uncle Ran's plan, was it?" I said.

Luca shook his head. "He always had to prove himself, always needed everyone to acknowledge he was the smartest person in the room. He was vicious if he didn't feel like he was properly respected." He finally took a slow sip. "And one day, I began to wonder how he'd really felt, working under Father."

The corner of his mouth quirked up. "For someone who thought he was the smartest man in the room, his personal data security was pretty loose."

I nearly spit out my drink. "You hacked his computers?"

Luca finally smiled, the mischief in his eyes replacing the seriousness. "Maybe?"

I leaned back against the pillows, feeling the almost imperceptible vibration of the station as we rotated in the blackness of the Void.

Nothing was what it seemed.

My quiet, dutiful, barely-older brother had been the rebel between the two of us, all along.

But the station was still here. And so were we.

"Alright, tell me what you found."

His mouth pursed, the facts more bitter than his tea. "Correspondence between Uncle and that woman, from long before she contacted Father."

Realization dawned. "It was a set-up from the beginning?"

Luca nodded, eyes closed, his shoulders finally relaxing.

This must've been the first time he'd been able to discuss his findings aloud, have anyone listen to him, believe him.

"It wasn't a suicide, was it?" I knew the answer. Just needed to hear someone else say it, make it real.

"No," he answered.

We stayed silent for a few minutes as I adjusted to the world changing yet again, the truth and the lies that had made up my life shifting and rearranging.

"I'm not going back with you," I said finally.

"What?"

Finally, I was the one to startle him.

"The corp has been my life for so long. Our life. I don't even know who I am without it."

Luca shook his head slowly. "Then what are you gonna do?"

"I don't know. But I want to find out."

Another chime of the door announced a visitor, and Luca's face broke into a grin. "I think I might have some ideas." He stood and nodded at Hakon, whose bulk filled the doorway. "I think I'll go see what our new friends are up to."

"Ronan's calmed down, if that's what you're asking," Hakon growled.

"That's reassuring," Luca answered as he left. "Has that crazy AI, though? I'm not sure which is scarier."

The door slid shut, but Hakon stayed on the far side of the room, his eyes searching my face for something.

"How are—"

"It wasn't that long ago you were shot through the

chest," I said. "If one more person asks me how I'm doing with a minor leg wound, I might scream."

"I see." The wary look left his face, and he moved closer.

"Or throw things," I continued. "And then I might really strain it."

"I wouldn't want that," he said, finally leaning over to kiss me.

His lips on mine tasted like home, his spicy scent a drug I'd never get enough of.

"At least I can think of better ways to make you scream," he murmured, his lips brushing my ear.

Winding my arms around his neck, I shifted my weight slightly and winced.

He pulled away reluctantly. "But I think we'll wait until Nadira says you're clear."

I sighed, flopping back. "It really doesn't hurt that much."

"I really don't want you to hurt at all, mate," he said, smoothing back my hair.

"Fine, then," I said, more than a little annoyed, and more than a lot frustrated. "Let's have a little talk."

You'd have thought I'd announced another attack on the station from how quickly Hakon straightened up. "A talk about what?"

"You've used that word a couple times now. What do

you mean?" I jabbed a finger at him. "Exactly. I'm not up for more surprises or secrets."

Hakon dragged the chair Luca had used closer to the bed and sat, his strong fingers caressing the back of my hand with surprising delicacy, but the heat in his gaze had no such restraint.

"Just what it sounds like. You're my mate. The only one for me."

Oh.

My chest tightened, throat closed, and I hoped he'd go on talking, because I wasn't sure I could answer.

Not yet, not while fighting through this wave of emotion.

Hakon took a deep breath, swallowed. "We should've talked about this before I shouted it across the room, but I couldn't help it." His hand stopped moving. "I don't know what your plans are, or where you're going next, but I know you're devoted to your family, your corporation. You have a life of your own."

I turned my hand over so I could trace patterns of my own on his palm. "When I thought my uncle had killed you," I started slowly, even that remembered pain was so much harder to bear than the inconsequential wound in my leg. "I realized a few things. I hadn't quite thought of you as my 'mate' yet," I smiled at the unfamiliar but somehow totally perfect expression. "But it felt like my heart had been ripped out and somehow I was expected to go on living. And when you strode across the hub, I knew how much I needed you, needed to be with you."

The words that had been pressing against my chest, ready to burst, finally came out. "I love you, and I'm not going anywhere without you."

That utterly charming smile transformed his face again, just as it had when I'd first seen him in the fabrication lab.

"I love you, too, my mate." Picking up my hand, he pressed a kiss to my palm, and my core quivered. Stupid leg.

"What do you want to do," he asked. "We have the whole galaxy to explore."

"First, I want to get out of this room," I decided, but at his scowl, I clarified. "Your friend Nadira said I couldn't put any weight on it. But I didn't think you'd mind carrying me?"

"There are a few things I like better," he admitted. "But those will have to wait."

Once I was securely in his arms, I snuggled into his chest. "Alright," I said, "take me somewhere new."

"I'll take you anywhere you want to go," and he strode off, only to stop by the door of the adjoining suite.

"Who's in here?" I asked.

"Everybody," he said. "Let me know if he gets too much."

The door slid open and I gasped. Somehow, while I'd been sedated some major construction had been going on. The suite had been expanded, furniture had been removed, and now a row of consoles lined the wall.

A dark-haired man, possibly even larger than Hakon, crossed the room to greet us. "You're looking better than the last time I saw you."

Nadira bustled up and elbowed him in the side. "That's not polite, babe. Most people don't like to be reminded of when they've been shot."

She rolled her eyes at him and leaned over to hug my shoulders lightly. "You'll get used to it, I hope. Their social skills are a little rough at times."

"Not all of us!" came a shout from the far corner where another of the giants was talking with Jenke.

"Torik, yours are worse than anyone's," Hakon called back. "You've been living in a cave for two years." He glanced down at me. "This is alright? Now that you're awake, I wanted you to meet everyone."

I nodded, torn between panic and overwhelming curiosity. "What are you guys doing here?" I said as Hakon, still holding me, carefully settled into one of the overstuffed chairs.

Ronan went back to one of the consoles, where it

looked like he was arguing with a small silver cube, but Nadira perched on the arm of another one of the chairs.

"Thalcorr is in the middle of negotiations with Mr. Alcyon and your brother," she explained. "After everything that's happened, Ronan decided it would be safer if we stuck around for a bit before heading for home." Her warm smile faltered as her eyes flickered between my face and Hakon's. "Unless I'm assuming too much."

I leaned back against Hakon's chest as his arms tightened around me. "I don't think so," I said. "But we might need to make a little detour."

I tilted my head up, pleased to see Hakon's look of surprise. "You did say you'd take me anywhere."

"And I meant it." He brushed my lips with his. "Going to let me know where?"

Gazing into his eyes, the noise and hustle of the room faded away, and we were alone, together.

"Maybe we could have a little time somewhere that wasn't trying to kill us," I murmured. "See how that feels."

"Sure you don't want to go test out that mushroom boat?" he teased. "Maybe go visit Bobo and his mom?"

"Don't tempt me," I answered, then found a better answer in the taste of his lips.

Finally, breathless, we broke apart.

"Mate," I said, finally at peace with the universe after too many years. "Let's go home."

"And where is that?" His hand cupped my cheek, and I smiled, basking in his warmth.

"Wherever you are," I answered. "That's home enough for me."

"For both of us," he insisted, and in his kiss, I felt the truth of it.

Forever.

PLEASE DON'T FORGET TO LEAVE A REVIEW!

Readers rely on your opinions, and your review can help others decide on what books they read. Make sure your opinion is heard and leave a review where you purchased this book!

Don't miss a new release! You can sign up for release alerts at both Amazon and Bookbub:

bookbub.com/authors/elin-wyn
amazon.com/author/elinwyn

For a free short story, opportunities for advance review copies, release news and the occasional cat picture, please join the newsletter!

https://elinwynbooks.com/newsletter-signup/

And don't forget the Facebook group, where I post sneak peeks of chapters and covers!

https://www.facebook.com/groups/ElinWyn/

NEED TO CATCH UP WITH THE STAR BREED?

Given: Star Breed Book One

When a renegade thief and a genetically enhanced mercenary collide, space gets a whole lot hotter!

Thief Kara Shimsi has learned three lessons well - keep her head down, her fingers light, and her tithes to the syndicate paid on time.

But now a failed heist has earned her a death sentence - a one-way ticket to the toxic Waste outside the dome. Her only chance is a deal with the syndicate's most ruthless enforcer, a wolfish mountain of genetically-modified muscle named Davien.

The thought makes her body tingle with dread-or is it heat?

Mercenary Davien has one focus: do whatever is necessary to get the credits to get off this backwater mining colony and back into space. The last thing he wants is a smart-mouthed thief - even if she does have the clue he needs to hunt down whoever attacked the floating lab he and his created brothers called home.

Caring is a liability. Desire is a commodity. And love could get you killed.

https://elinwynbooks.com/star-breed/

DON'T MISS THE CONQUERED
WORLD!

He shattered her world. Can she trust him with her heart?

Giant spiders, walking trees, bloodthirsty vines.

For Jeneva, it's just another day trying to survive in the jungles of Ankau.

Until the sky ripped open, and the true monsters came through.

Now her world is under attack, and the only place of safety may be at the side of a rock-hard scaled alien.

But he's filled with secrets - how can she trust him?

Vrehx cares for nothing other than the destruction of the Xathi hordes who burned his home and killed his family.

But when a weapons test goes horribly wrong, the battle spills over to an uncharted world.

The planet is filled with lethal native life...but nothing is more dangerous than the human woman who obsesses his thoughts.

When war rages around them, can they fight together, or will his burning need for her drive them apart?

Vrehx is the first book in the science fiction romance series Conquered World. Each book is a new romance with alpha male alien warriors and women who don't put up with their nonsense. No cheating, no cliffhangers, HEA guaranteed!

Click to get Vrehx now or keep reading for a sample!
https://elinwynbooks.com/conquered-world-alien-romance/

VREHX

Streaks of plasma lit the blackness as a squadron of Valorni fighters swooped in dizzying spirals, blasting at the massive Xathi ship that filled the screens of the *Vengeance*.

We were so close it was the size of a planet. Like two steel ziggurats smashed and welded together. Not practical for space flight, but efficient enough to tear through several worlds.

Designed to intimidate.

Designed to destroy.

And we were going to stop it.

We crept closer, waiting. I sucked in my breath, geared for the inevitable.

I gritted my teeth as the bridge shook, and Karzin let out an undignified whoop from his station on the far curve of the bridge. The purple stripes on his shoulders rippled, and his excited eyes darted back and forth as if cheering on his favorite sport.

Barbarian. His crude Valorni traits got on my last nerve—not that he gave a rat's ass. Like the lot of them, he had no empathy for others. He barely listened to commands and forget anyone who didn't at least match his rank.

"You green motherfuckers aren't supposed to be hitting us, just laying cover for our approach," I snarled. "They can remember that much, can't they?"

They had only begun venturing into space when we took them into the alliance, but surely they weren't that stupid.

I hoped not.

"Fuck you," the Valorni drawled. The stretched-out

sounds of his abominable accent were like bristles to my red Skotan scales. "Not their fault we're cloaked all to hell."

What an asshole. Valorni couldn't even be bothered to speak accurately. Their drawl made it nearly impossible to understand them, and they had idiotic slang for everything.

"They were informed of our flight path before the battle." The lights of Sk'lar's implants flickered in the dim light of the bridge. "It should have been simple for them to avoid it."

I smiled just a little, glad I wasn't the only one with some common sense. Sk'lar wasn't much better than Karzin, but he was more tolerable. My biggest problem was his implants.

His artificial augmentation was just creepy and wrong. You could see them light up in biohazard green against his shiny black skin. He looked like a fucking motherboard.

The strike team leaders were chosen for their specific talents and leadership, but Sk'lar's was not stealth outside the ship.

Karzin made it a point to butt heads with all of us. That usually distracted the rest of us from being at each other's throats.

Maybe that was his intention. Whatever. He was an asshole.

Karzin shrugged off the K'ver's barely concealed criticism. "Not gonna matter in a few minutes, is it?"

The sarcasm warranted him a disapproving side-eye from Sk'lar, which he ignored. I hated to admit it, but the jackass was right. In a few minutes, we would probably all be dead.

"Gentlemen," Rouhr's quiet word from the command station silenced the chatter, "are you prepared?"

The scar that ran down the left side of his face rippled as he clenched his jaw. He was annoyed.

Of course, we were prepared.

We shut up anyway. Rouhr was very diplomatic. That's why he was in charge.

We straightened ourselves and regained our concentration.

Tension and anger clogged the air, but there was no fear. Fear had died when our families did, when our worlds had burned under the Xathi attacks.

Around the half circle, each of us activated the new weapons panels, the long seconds drawing out as they lit up and hummed. Every battle had this moment—the waiting before the storm.

But this would be different.

We owned the storm.

"Let's blow a hole in those bastards," I growled, eyes

fixed on the sickly green hull, thinking of the swarms inside.

They waited for the go ahead to surge through over the squadrons like locusts.

Nothing had been able to penetrate a Xathi hiveship before. They just plowed through and destroyed whatever they wanted, the swarms mopping up whatever the hiveship missed.

The Valorni, as annoying as they were, were inducted into the alliance for one reason. The Sugavians had worked with K'ver scientists using codialite, a mineral from the Valorni homeworld, to make one last attempt.

Just enough had been mined for this last-ditch effort —an experimental weapon that had a shot at penetrating that hull. It was rare, and we were on the losing end of this fight. We only had one shot.

We'd better make it count.

Every Skotan, K'ver, and Valorni warrior on the *Vengeance* had volunteered in the knowledge that it was a one-way trip. If this worked, the three strike teams below would board the Xathi and battle until there was nothing left.

If it didn't, we'd all die—just sooner.

Either way, the recorder satellites would beam the results of the experiment back to the scientists and engineers. We'd succeed, or they'd build a better weapon next time. That was the most important part of the mission, and we all understood how expendable we were.

The three of us locked focus on our stations as we crept closer.

"We are now in firing range, Captain," Sk'lar reported.

"Fire at will," was the only response.

Karzin sent the signal to the Valorni ships, and I started a slow count.

One.

His comrades had fought stupidly but bravely. There was no discernable pattern to the attack.

I was worried more would take friendly fire than would hit the Xathi, but they somehow made sense of the chaos, dodging fire from their comrades. If any survived the battle, they deserved to escape.

Two.

More likely the crazy bastards would follow us into the breach, but they'd earned the choice.

Three.

I activated the launch panel and braced, eyes fixed on the monitors. The adrenaline rushed through me in anticipation of the blow.

Nothing.

Not a bang or a pop or a whine. Just the hum of the

engines, and the wall of the Xathi ship growing larger on the screens.

The anticipation deflated as I looked at the panel in confusion. The damn thing was experimental, but it should at least fire. The engineers weren't brain-dead.

With a snarl, I slapped it again.

And then the universe turned inside out.

JENEVA

I was in my element.

I was where I belonged.

Completely alone in the silence, except for the gigantic bipedal tree creature with an affinity for spewing poison.

Home sweet home.

A glob of the foul stuff hissed as it ate away the earth beneath me. It was only inches from my boot, but I didn't flinch or try to move out of the way.

A rapid movement around a sorvuc was far more dangerous than its projectile poison. Its damn branches were covered in tiny neural fibers, capable of detecting incredibly small movements. The fibers were illuminated purple.

The sorvuc searched for me.

Under different circumstances, I would have found

it beautiful, but at that moment, it was just a pain in my ass.

The humidity made my short hair damp and scratchy. It clung to the curve of my neck. I longed to brush it away, but a movement like that would be a death sentence.

The luminescent purple faded away to a tranquil pink. I realized I was holding my breath.

Slowly, so slowly, I crept closer to the wide trunk of the sorvuc. I had already made an incision in its trunk. That's what pissed it off in the first place.

A necessary risk, but I only needed a few more drops of the thick scarlet fluid that seeped from the incision. The right person would pay a small fortune for its sap—or is it blood? Hell if I know.

As I slid my vial into place, ready to collect the liquid the sale of which would keep me comfortable for months, shouts erupted from somewhere nearby.

Damn it.

The sorvuc shrieked, its neural fibers flaring purple once again. It pivoted, razor-sharp leaves dangerously close to me. I rolled away, camouflaging my own movements in its rustling.

The hulking creature lumbered off in the direction the shouts came from—sort of. Its neural fibers must have picked up the sound vibrations, but with so many trees, it would have been difficult for the creature to determine the exact direction.

It's a good thing sorvuc had those fibers. They were as deaf as, well, a tree—at least, the sort of trees our ancestors brought over on their generation ship. But those trees sure as hell didn't fling poison or walk.

Walking plants were something the dense forest of Ankau had in excess. Even so, I'd take a hostile tree giant over people any day. At least they left me in peace.

Another round of shouts echoed through the trees. I clenched my teeth.

Speaking of peace.

I moved quickly and quietly through the dense forest, mindful not to disturb any of the thick vines that crisscrossed the forest floor. It was difficult to tell which ones were looking for a snack.

I spied a small herd of luurizi grazing between the roots of the docile Lenaus trees.

Their coats of lilac, sage, and pearl shimmered when they caught the mottled light bleeding through the canopy. Their silvery horns shone like jewels. It was easy to forget how deadly they were.

I was sure they could smell me.

Ordinarily, they would attack the moment they sensed an intruder. But this particular herd had become accustomed to my scent after so many years. It was an uneasy truce, but I still knew better than to take my eye off them.

Another bout of shouting brought me back to the present. It was louder this time. And stupider.

Clearly, whoever it was had a death wish, which was fine. I'd just prefer to be farther away when it happened.

The trees gave way to a small clearing. Two women, who I can only assume are the shouting morons, stood inches away from each other, their faces red with anger. They didn't notice my intrusion.

"You're not even trying anymore!" One woman, blonde and petite, hissed at the other. Her voice was tight, like she was trying to stay in control.

Sharp would have been the only way to describe her —sharp cheekbones, sharp chin, and sharp shoulders. Even her mouth was a sharp slash across her face.

I winced at her words, a headache throbbing at my temples. I almost wished something *would* come along and kill them.

"What more do you want me to do?" The other woman, dark-haired and softer than the other, answered wearily. "If I had known you were going to bring this up, I never would have agreed to meet you!"

Though they were different in coloring, they had the same nose and face shape. I guessed they were sisters—not that I cared.

"What other reason would there be to meet up?" the blonde snapped, her gray-green eyes narrowing. "What else do we have anymore?"

There was more poison in those words than there was in a fully grown sorvuc.

"I hate to interrupt," I said, startling both women.

I wanted to sound as annoyed as I felt, but my voice was brittle and raspy with disuse. I couldn't even remember the last time I had spoken aloud.

"But you really should shut up," I continued.

The blonde pivoted to face me. I was at least a head taller than her, but she somehow seemed bigger than she actually was. And the glare on her face would have made a narrisiri hesitate.

"This is none of your business," she said through clenched teeth.

"Nope, it isn't. I don't want to know about it. I don't care about it. But you really should find somewhere else to finish your screaming match," I replied.

"Do you think we're idiots? We have a howler with us," the blonde smugly fished a small black device from her pocket.

I hated those damn things. They emitted a high-pitched sound above the threshold of human hearing. It was meant to repel the creatures that stalked the forest, but I always thought it was a scam.

First of all, the people living in the cities and towns

hardly knew anything about the creatures that lived out here in the forest. Second, how would anyone know for a fact that a howler was working? No one could hear it.

"Yes, I do think you're idiots if you think that carrying a howler into the middle of aramirion territory during nesting season is a good idea," I snapped, fighting the urge to give the blonde a smug smile. "If they can hear that thing, you're screwed."

The dark-haired woman paled as she put her hand on the blonde's shoulder. The blonde stiffened at her touch.

"Leena, is that true?" the dark-haired woman whispered. Her eyes, the same color as the blonde's, nervously scanned the surrounding forest.

"How the hell would I know, Mariella? You're the one who moved all the way out to the middle of freaking nowhere!" the blonde, Leena, grumbled.

I turned to leave. Obviously, they had no intention of listening to me. Perhaps the dark-haired one, Mariella, might have seen reason, but Leena had some sort of chip on her shoulder—a chip the size of a damn ravine.

Fine. Whatever. They were adults.

I'd tried my best to warn them. It's not my fault if they chose not to listen to me.

What would I know, right? I've only been living out here for fifteen years. They would come to their senses and leave, or they would keep at it until one beast or another silenced them.

Either way, I got my forest and my silence back.

I could still feel their flurries of emotion as I marched through the undergrowth. If I was going to find another sorvuc to fill my vial, I needed to concentrate, but I couldn't do that with the feelings of two idiots in my head. I should turn back, try even harder to get them to leave.

A horrible screech unlike anything I had ever heard tore through the air. The sheer force of it drove me to my knees.

I tried to protect my ears with my hands, but it was useless. My vision blurred, stars danced behind my eyelids. I could practically feel my brain thrashing, desperate to escape that terrible sound.

Those idiots either did something to their howler, or the damn thing was malfunctioning. That had to be it.

As soon as I could get back on my feet, I staggered back to the clearing where I'd left the arguing pair. I would tear their stupid howler apart with my bare hands if I had to—anything to stop the noise.

"What the hell did you do?" I yelled.

Again, they didn't notice me when I entered the clearing, but, this time, they weren't distracted by an argument.

They stood side by side, looking up at the sky. Their faces were pale and their mouths were open in terror and confusion. I followed their gaze.

A jagged scar of pitch marred the once pristine stretch of endless blue.

The sky, *my* sky, had been torn open.

There was a beat of silence as if the whole planet had drawn in a collective breath of shock.

Then the forest erupted into chaos.

VREHX

Alarms blared around us. On the screen, all I could see were swirls of colors swallowing the Xathi.

The captain shouted orders to the rest of the crew, but his voice was distorted. It was changing—high-pitched then low and deep, fast then robotic, child-like then old, clear and loud, then soft and unintelligible.

Looking around the bridge, some of the colors were vibrant, glowing, and bright. Others were non-existent, as if all color had been drained, leaving behind various shades of gray.

Karzin's face twisted, melting down toward his midsection. I wanted to vomit, but Karzin's bird-like voice was chirping at me.

"TURN! IT! OFF!"

I turned my attention back to my control panel, just

to see it swirl around and fade. The screen was so bright, my eyes burned. The letters seemed to be dancing an old Skotan wedding march.

Looking up at the screen, the Xathi ship was ripped apart by the swirling vortex—no, it wasn't a vortex.

It was just a hole. Then it was a rip.

The only thing that stayed the same were the colors. Purple, white, and red streaks of color were covering the Xathi ship and reaching out for us.

The part of the Xathi ship already inside the rip was separating, coming apart at the seams. I could see part of the Xathi crew floating in space, then shredded by the force of the rip.

And we were getting closer to it.

I heard Rouhr's voice yelling out commands, for the engine room to go full speed ahead and drive the Xathi ship further into the rip.

It made sense. If the rip was doing this kind of damage to the "top" half, then it should destroy the rest of it as well. If we went with it, so be it.

The engines kicked in, and we were rocked forward as we crashed the *Vengeance* into the Xathi ziggurat. Our momentum pushed the Xathi ship further into the rip, and I watched as more and more of their vessels were ripped and disintegrated. It was only a few short breaths before the *Vengeance* herself began to fall through.

The energy inside her was incredible. The air carried a charge that made my scales tighten and my hair stand on end. Every color I had ever seen exploded in my eyes, bringing me a level of pain I had never felt before.

My mouth opened to scream, but no sound came out. It was as if my throat was burning and ripping in half vertically. I felt my skin and scales peel away from my body, exposing my muscles and bones to the emptiness of the void.

My eyelids, clamped as tight as I could hold them, broke apart and fell away, slowly exposing my eyes to the grayness of the void we had entered.

The bridge of the *Vengeance* was a bright gray, and everything else was varying shades of gray, getting darker and darker.

I looked at Rouhr to see his body falling apart like sand. He was yelling at us, but there was no sound.

That's when I realized that there was no sound at all. There wasn't a single solitary noise. Was the rip in space this quiet or had my ears been destroyed?

I moved my hand to touch my ear and stared in wonder at the stump at the end of my arm. I looked down, and my fingers were on my lap.

I wanted to retch. I wanted to die. I wanted to close my damn eyes.

I looked up at the screen to see the ziggurat, at least

the second half that we were attached to, reconstitute itself. It was rebuilding!

Then we were rebuilding, and the first of my senses to return was feeling. The pain was so much that I should have blacked out, except my eyelids weren't there.

When they finally returned, and I blinked for the first time, tears fell down my face. Finally, sound came back with an explosion of noise.

"...the hell is happening?"

"...are we?"

"Damage reports!"

"...off the damn switch."

"...switch, Vrehx!"

It felt as though forever was passing before my mind caught on to what they were wanting. I looked at my control panel and flipped the switch to the weapon. The void ended, and the alarms were back.

"Where the hell are we?" Rouhr asked.

"I'm not sure, Captain!" Sk'lar answered.

"Scan the—" Rouhr was interrupted as the ship shook violently, knocking most of us from our seats. "By all that is holy, what was that?"

Engineer Thribb's voice came on over the intercom. "We're losing engines, Captain. Partial power only. We've been caught by a gravitational field of some sort."

"What is generating the field?"

"I'm not sure, sir. My systems are inoperative."

"Sk'lar!"

"On it!" Sk'lar checked his system, letting out a curse that the translator didn't bother to translate. There was no need. "We're above a planet. Unfortunately, we are falling toward it."

He tried to keep his voice calm, but the slight vibrato betrayed his emotions.

The *Vengeance* wasn't built for the atmosphere of a planet. Our thrusters wouldn't work. If we fell into the atmosphere of a planet, we'd fall until we impacted with the ground, and it would be a very hard landing.

"Sir! The Xathi!" I called out, pointing at the screen.

The Xathi ziggurat was tilting, as if it were falling as well. Outside scanners adjusted and brought the full picture into view.

The planet was covered in green and blue, and above it, the Xathi ship tilted ever more as it fell.

"What planet is this, and where are the Xathi going to land?" Rouhr asked.

I brought up our positioning and the star maps in our database. "Sir, this is uncharted space for us. We don't have this planet or this system in our database."

Rouhr nodded, absorbing the information. "Crash site?"

Sk'lar turned to look at me, then at Rouhr. The look

on his face was silent resignation that something bad was going to happen.

"There appear to be seven main points of population on the planet. The Xathi are going to crash into the biggest concentration," Sk'lar said.

"Estimated survival?"

"Not good. Easily half of their city will be destroyed, killing thousands."

"And what of the Xathi? Will they survive the crash?"

"I'm not sure, sir. I'm not sure what the interior makeup of their vessel is, so I couldn't give you an accurate guess," Sk'lar replied, refusing to look at Rouhr as he stared at the computer.

"Engineer Thribb?"

"Captain?"

"Any chance of us breaking free and *not* crashing on the planet below?"

"Less than three percent, sir."

"Well, *groop*." We all looked at Rouhr in shock. "Any way to get us away from civilization?"

"Easily, as long as our engines don't finish cutting out on the way down."

"Then keep us away from any population centers. The rest of you, brace for impact!"

We watched the Xathi ziggurat crash into the center

city, the largest city, as we strapped ourselves into our seats.

The cloud of dust and flame took out half of our sensors as we entered the atmosphere. We gained speed and tilted forward, and I could feel the pressure of the straps trying to hold me up as gravity pulled me downward.

It was a struggle to breathe. The pull of gravity was forcing us downward, while the atmosphere tried to resist our penetration. I tried to lift my arm to my console to push the button for the retro rockets in order to level us out and slow us down, but I couldn't lift my arm high enough.

The ground rushed at us, and I closed my eyes.

I'll be back with you soon, my family, I thought. My only hope was that we took those bastards with us.

My head snapped forward as the *Vengeance* crashed into the ground.

There was no way that death could possibly hurt this much.

I looked to my left to see Karzin slowly and gingerly lifting his head. Just past him, S'toz's head hung forward, his chin on his chest. To my right, Sk'lar was moaning in pain, trying to reach his arm up to his head.

I slowly—oh, so, so slowly reached up to unbuckle my straps. Now free from my restraints—and oh so grateful for them, as well—I gingerly got to my feet, waiting for the blast of pain to overwhelm my senses.

"Location?" I asked.

Sk'lar answered after a short coughing fit. "We're planet-side. That's all I know. Last thing I remember seeing was that we were heading for a large forest."

That's when it finally hit me. The computers were down.

"Captain?"

A groan from behind Sk'lar answered us. Rouhr's straps had snapped, and he ended up being flung around.

"I'm still alive. Vrehx?" He pulled himself to a sitting position on the floor, his right arm dangling, blood flowing from his cheek, and his left arm clutching his ribs.

"Sir?" My left arm hurt, and it was hard to breathe, I might have cracked a rib or six. I had a headache from the depths of destruction, and I was struggling to maintain weight on my right ankle.

"Get the commanders and your teams together. Find out where we are and if we're in danger. Thribb and I will handle the ship."

I knew better than to argue with him.

I made my way to the lift, but the doors wouldn't open.

DON'T MISS THE CONQUERED WORLD!

I moved three steps to my left and opened the maintenance hatch. Looking down, it was surprisingly clear.

Time to climb, I thought.

At least it was downward.

Click to get Vrehx now!

https://elinwynbooks.com/conquered-world-alien-romance/

I love old movies – *To Catch a Thief, Notorious, All About Eve* — and anything with Katherine Hepburn in it. Clever, elegant people doing clever, elegant things.

I'm a hopeless romantic.

And I love science fiction and the promise of space.

So it makes perfect sense to me to try to merge all of those loves into a new science fiction world, where dashing heroes and lovely ladies have adventures, get into trouble, and find their true love in the stars!

www.ingramcontent.com/pod-product-compliance
Lightning Source LLC
Chambersburg PA
CBHW070737180626
46818CB00007B/2890